Other books by Kyell Gold:

Volle
Pendant of Fortune
The Prisoner's Release and Other Stories
Waterways
Out of Position
Shadow of the Father
Isolation Play
Weasel Presents
Green Fairy
The Silver Circle
Divisions
Red Devil (coming 2014)

X (editor)

Other Cupcakes:

The Peculiar Quandary of Simon Canopus Artyle, by Rikoshi
Science Friction, by Kyell Gold
Dangerous Jade, by foozzzball
Winter Games, by Kyell Gold

Order at FurPlanet.com or scan the code below:

BRIDGES

by Kyell Gold

BRIDGES

Copyright 2010, 2013 by Kyell Gold

Published by FurPlanet
Dallas, Texas
http://www.furplanet.com

ISBN 978-1-61450-123-7
Printed in the United States of America
First trade paperback edition: February 2010
Second trade paperback edition: June 2013

Cover art and interior illustrations by Keovi

For K.M. Hirosaki, who inspired this story

And for Kit, who inspires me every day

CONTENTS

Seriously, Amir thought, *how the hell do people meet each other?*

He was sitting in a chair in the Foxed Page, a bookstore in the Riverwalk district of the city of Gateway, a new Elthia Jones mystery lying forgotten in his lap. Across the Mystery and Science Fiction room of the sprawling indie bookstore, a vixen he'd come to recognize over the past two months was chatting animatedly with a well-dressed red fox he'd only seen this past week. Somehow, mysteriously, the two of them had formed a connection.

The Foxed Page certainly had a comfortable, intimate atmosphere that Amir thought would be conducive to hooking up, which is why he'd taken to spending every afternoon there. The old townhouse had been barely modified, leaving the staircases up to the second and third floors still narrow; the shelves of books faced overstuffed couches that were perfect for squeezing into the corners of. Sitting with his tail curled around his knees, Amir felt like he was visiting someone's grandmother— an interesting grandmother, engaging, who would make you cookies and loan you books and wink at you and your boyfriend, not the kind who would put plastic on all the furniture and eye you suspiciously when you looked too long at any of her possessions and make you and your boyfriend sit on separate chairs.

What's more, The Foxed Page shared space with Under Grounds, a coffee shop that had weak coffee but excellent masala chai, and they let you take the chai up into the bookstore. The store and coffee shop also had an eclectic, fascinating clientele—mostly foxes, which made him feel a little more relaxed. More than half the time he spent in the store, he only pretended to read a book while he watched the chubby red fox scan the poetry section and stop with a gasp at one of the new releases, or the stocky arctic fox who stood leaning against the literature section reading the back of every book on the shelf at his eye level, or the vixen, the one who'd just met someone, perusing the travel section with audible sniffs of condescension.

If there had been bookstores like this back home, he might not have—definitely would not have—spent so much time in bars there. So although he knew how to hit on a cute guy in a bar, he really had no idea how to approach someone in a bookstore. He just knew that the chances of meeting someone he'd want to get to know were way better here than at home, and better in a bookstore than at a bar.

Craning his neck, he could see the vixen and her tod in the travel section, where she was showing him some books without a single condescending sniff. He caught snatches of their conversation: "love to go sometime..." "...beautiful place, the people were so nice..."

Amir took refuge from his might-as-well-not-be-heated apartment (the landlord seemed to think that fennec fur was just as good as red fox fur, even though Amir's winter coat was half as thick as the reds he knew) in the couches of The Foxed Page often enough that the regulars had had plenty of time to recognize him as one of their own. The chubby red fox who liked poetry was there almost every day Amir was, and there was an arctic fox whose jewelry was as ostentatious as his aloof attitude. But none of them showed any interest in getting to know Amir better. He knew how to buy a guy a drink in a bar, a tenuous connection that usually lasted only until both of them had come, but here, he was lost. How the hell did people make things last? He had contemplated running down to the coffee shop to buy a coffee for the more interesting guys, but he didn't know how to ask them what they wanted, and since he himself didn't like Under Grounds' coffee, it didn't seem worth the risk. Lion Christ, he'd tell himself after letting each opportunity slip by, it's not like you moved to Gateway just to meet someone, right? Right?

As the newly-happy couple left, Amir sat back in his couch. Maybe he should try answering some of the personal ads in the alternative paper. He didn't want to be that desperate, but it was that or the bars; nothing else was working. There were ten or eleven other students in his grad school cohort—all, so far as he could determine, either straight or asexual.

When he'd moved to the city to work toward an advanced degree, he'd resolved that he was going to grow up, that he didn't want to spend his whole life in one-night stands as an infrequent diversion from his tired paw. But this whole "hang out where people you'd be interested in would hang out" thing clearly wasn't working out for him. Or maybe he was just so horny right now that he was feeling more desperate than usual. Either way, it felt like it would take some kind of divine intervention to get him a date, much less a boyfriend.

All right, he told himself. Give the mystery another chapter and then hit a bar on the way home. At least get a drink. And if there's a cute guy there...especially if he's a fox...maybe just once.

Before he could even open his book, though, his large ears pricked up. He had become familiar with the low humming of one particular red fox, who'd only been coming to the bookstore for a couple weeks, and who intrigued Amir more than any of the other patrons. For one thing, this fox wore tight jeans and an open vest—he must leave his overcoat at the counter. Unlike most of the patrons of the bookstore, he was tightly muscled and almost hyperactive, bouncing on his feet even when standing still. His tail twitched when it wasn't swishing, and his ears flicked constantly around, as though he were paranoid someone was sneaking up on him. But the few times Amir had seen his expression, he'd never looked scared or worried. He always wore a faint smile, as if he'd just come from or were just going to see a lover and was cherishing the memory or the anticipation.

And, most intriguing of all, his taste in books seemed to vary wildly from one day to the next. Juvenile fantasy gave way to Social Psychology, which was replaced by a hard-boiled crime thriller. Amir was an avid reader, but even he hadn't bounced between so many genres so quickly.

Well, to be honest, the *most* intriguing features of the fox were the tight, rounded curves under his tail, and the flowing way that tail arched and swung behind him. Just from looking at it, Amir had no doubt that that tail had been lifted many times, and the more he thought about it, especially today, the more glad he was that he had a book concealing his lap.

This time, a book of Sudoku puzzles dangled loosely beside that sweetly rounded rear. Amir let his gaze linger. Definitely was going to need at least a paw tonight. Might be better than a bar, actually. If he tried to pick up someone, as frustrated as he felt now, it'd not be very good. If only he could just walk up to this fox and say, "hey, can I get you a coffee?"

Don't kid yourself, he told himself glumly. The fox would look him over and say, "thanks, but I'm set." He'd leave, and Amir wouldn't even have the daydreams about him anymore. They were such nice daydreams, too, he didn't want to give them up. He watched the fox's rear swing from side to side, the long red tail flowing behind it, almost mesmerizing...and then the fox turned his head and looked right back at him.

Amir felt his large ears flush. He folded them down and buried his nose in the thriller, trying to pick up the flow of the text again, but as the police lieutenant in his text talked about the grisly crime scene, all Amir

saw was the red fox's clear golden eyes, the little fang at the edge of his muzzle, the slight curve of his smile. God, staring in a public bookstore like a horny little fag who hadn't even had an ear-nibble in months. What was wrong with him?

Maybe, he thought, what was wrong with him was that he *was* a horny little fag who hadn't even had an ear-nibble in months. That thought was swiftly followed by another brief daydream about the red fox's slender muzzle in his large ear, tongue licking up the edge, sharp teeth nibbling at the skin. He could almost feel the warm breath ruffling the short fur, his whole body tingling as it did. He knew fairly well what the red would smell like; he imagined that musk thicker in his nostrils, the nose pushing gently deeper against his inner ear...

Any hope he had of getting further in his book was gone. Time to go home, or at least down to the coffee shop. His chai had run out half an hour ago, anyway.

"That's a pretty good book," someone said softly right next to him, right into the soft fur of his left ear.

He almost jumped out of the couch. Turning, he saw the red fox bending over, paws on his knees so his muzzle was at Amir's ear level. He was grinning a cocky grin, and Amir could just see the swish of his tail behind him. He'd come around the other way, through the poetry room and around to the doorway behind the couch. "You surprised me," Amir said, composing himself.

"Oh, I'm sorry." The red straightened and pointed at the book. "I saw you reading it. I was reading it last week."

Amir nodded. "It's pretty good. I mean, so far," he said. The guy was just standing there, still grinning, so Amir took a breath and a chance. "My name's Amir," he said.

"You look like an 'Amir,'" the red said. "I don't see many fennecs this far north."

Amir brought his ears up. "I just moved here. For school."

The fox raised an eyebrow. "Pinewood?"

"Graduate school," Amir clarified.

"Ah, that makes more sense." The red sat on the corner of the couch. "I'm Hayward, but my friends just call me "Hay.""

"Hay?"

"As in, 'hey you.'" He chuckled, and extended a paw. "It's a pleasure to meet'cha, Amir. Welcome to Gateway." As Amir shook, he went on. "How do you like it so far?"

"It's cold." Amir grinned. "Sorry, but it is."

"No argument." Hayward leaned back slightly, letting the left edge of his vest fall away from his bare chest. The sleek fur in muscular lines distracted Amir for a moment. "Usually we only get a couple cold snaps like this a winter. You get used to it. You from the southwest?"

Amir nodded. "Viyajo. It's about two hours south of Chevali."

"I know a guy in Chevali," Hayward said. "Never been there myself."

"Did you grow up here?"

Hayward started to answer, then looked around the bookstore. "You need more tea? Want to head down to the café?"

They sat at a table together in the café talking for another hour. It was impossible to guess Hayward's age, and Amir didn't ask; the red fox had no grey on his muzzle or ears, and hadn't started to thicken around the middle. He could've been anywhere between twenty and thirty-five. His black-furred fingers tapped his coffee cup as he talked, or his foot tapped the floor, or his ears flicked around like radar dishes, or all three at the same time. He took his coffee with caramel syrup and extra milk, and when Amir'd said that it wasn't really coffee any more then, he'd said, "that's the idea." He talked easily and fluidly on any number of topics, and half his stories included the phrase, "Oh, I know someone who..." He knew the owners of the café and the bookstore; he knew a professor at Pinewood College; he knew a wolf who played on the Gateway hockey team; and he knew two of the tenors in the Gay League Chorus.

Amir perked up his ears at that. Hayward saw, and grinned. "You didn't really doubt, did you?" he said, leaving just a little tongue showing at the tip of his muzzle.

"Not really." Amir still hadn't figured out why the lively red fox was interested in him, but the length of time they'd spent talking emboldened him. He looked around out of habit, but none of the large vulpine ears in the café were turned their way. "I figured it would be too much of a tragedy to waste that body on vixens."

The moment he said it, he cursed himself for using a bar line on this fox. But Hayward laughed, looking pleased, and Amir's sense of the fragility of the moment passed. "And I knew from the way you were looking at me."

Amir folded his ears down. "Sorry."

"Don't be. I wouldn't dress like this if I didn't want to be appreciated." He leaned a little closer. "So, you moved up here on your own? No boyfriend waiting in Viyajo?"

"God, no." Amir snorted. "The guys in Viyajo are basically cretins. There's exactly one gay bar and the most eligible guy there is..." He stopped, hardly able to believe what he'd been about to say.

"Is...?"

"Uh...no offense, but I just met you." Amir felt his ears flushing again. He stuck his muzzle in his cup and sipped some chai.

Hayward said, "Hey," and when Amir looked up, the red fox was grinning. "You don't have to. But I'll tell you about this skunk I picked up one time at a bar. He was half-drunk and insisted we go back to his place. Which turned out to be a hotel room at one of the seediest places in Dellwood—that's the town about two miles that way, and picking the seediest hotel in Dellwood is like picking the filthiest stall in a train station men's room. And then it wasn't even his hotel room."

"So what'd you do?"

Hayward's voice was almost a purr. "Well, we fucked in the hallway."

Amir nearly spit tea back into his cup. He coughed and sputtered. "You didn't!"

"It was three in the morning and it didn't take that long. And half the lights were out anyway."

"Did anyone...I mean, did you..."

"Get caught? Nah. Well, *I* didn't. *I* got a good lay and then pulled up my pants and left him snoring on the carpet."

Amir stared. Who *was* this fox? "Seriously."

Hayward traced his fingers over his bare chest. "Cross my heart." He leaned forward again. "So, knowing that, would you be interested in having some dinner?"

Amir squinted. "Is that your worst story?"

"Honey," Hayward said, "it isn't even in the top ten."

"Well, then, how can I say no?" Amir grinned.

⊢⊣

Hayward gave him directions to a Mediterranean place two blocks over, and a time three hours away, enough for Amir to go home and stare at his closet for half an hour, wondering what he could wear to his first date in a new city. He settled for a nice collared shirt, and his best pair of slacks, which also had the advantage of being fairly thin and good for groping, should the evening progress that far. Which, when he thought about it, wasn't in much more doubt than Hayward's preferences.

It still worried him that an obviously outgoing, confident fox would hit on a bookish fennec curled up in a couch in a bookstore. Especially after the story of the skunk in the hotel. But Hayward was undeniably interested in him, and Amir was damn sure going to find out why. Maybe he wasn't boyfriend material—Amir spent an anxious minute wondering how he would deal with Hayward's flirtiness if he were a boyfriend—but Amir knew couples that were odder than he and Hayward would make. So he'd keep an open mind, and, if it came to it, muzzle.

He shivered his way back to the restaurant, getting there five minutes early. He wasn't surprised to see Hayward already sitting at a small table against the wall, sipping from a glass of water, wearing the same open vest and tight jeans, a body-length navy blue coat slung over the back of his chair. The surprise was that he wasn't alone: a tall swift fox sat across the table, talking with him.

Amir's heart sank. Maybe Hayward was the kind of guy who made a bunch of dates in case one didn't show up, and it was first-come, first-served. He'd known Hayward was too outgoing and popular a guy to really be interested in him.

Or, he thought, nudging himself mentally, maybe the swift fox was just a friend Hayward had run into. He knew a lot of people, after all. So maybe he was just killing time until Amir showed up. But should he just walk over there?

He didn't have to make the decision. Hayward spotted him and raised a paw, calling across the restaurant, "Amir!"

Tail wagging, reassured, Amir padded between the small tables and other diners and made his way to Hayward's table. The red fox waved him to the third chair as the swift fox stood, revealing cotton slacks to go with his blue collared shirt and brown vest. "Amir," Hayward said, "this is Fin. Sorry—Ruffin."

"Fin is fine." The swift fox had a deeper voice than either Amir or Hayward. He held out a dusty-brown paw with black streaks on the back. Amir shook it, and as he sat down, so did Fin.

Amir looked uncertainly at Hayward, who smiled back. "Fin's a friend of mine from the community theater. *Much Ado About Nothing*, last summer. I saw him outside and it turned out he wasn't doing anything for dinner. I figured it'd be good for you to meet a few more people. Amir's just moved up here from near Chevali," he said to Fin.

Fin asked him how he liked it, so Amir said something automatic about the weather while he struggled to understand what was going on. Granted, he hadn't been on many dates, but he'd been on a few, and he knew that by and large, one didn't invite third parties along. "Oh...city planning," he said, when Fin asked what he was studying.

"Ah, Pinewood's good for that," Fin said, and it turned out he knew an architect in downtown Gateway who'd gotten his degree from Pinewood. And after that, Amir asked about the play Fin was currently in, as they all chewed warm pita bread with hummus. Fin had a lot of entertaining stories about actors, which Amir could sympathize with from his English classes, although Fin's stories were a bit dirtier. Hayward seemed perfectly happy telling even dirtier stories about Fin, and it was Fin who was more interested in Amir's Habitat for the Homeless work. By the time the fragrant, spiced chicken arrived for the main course, Amir was having a little trouble remembering exactly who he was on the date with.

Until he caught a look from Hayward. Glancing to his right, he saw the red fox's tail flicking back and forth. Fin was trying to flag down a waiter to get a dessert order, and Hayward slid Amir a sly wink. When Fin looked back, Hayward coughed and stood up. "I'm going to hit the head," he said. "Be right back."

"Sure." Fin turned to talk to the waiter, a tall coyote in a gold-trimmed white vest.

Hayward's tail brushed Amir's leg as he walked away. Amir glanced up and saw the other jerk his muzzle in an unmistakable "follow me" gesture.

Really? Amir glanced back at Fin, who was asking the waiter whether the baklava had walnuts. Amir was intrigued that he liked baklava, but the invitation of Hayward's swinging tail and hips, luring him to the back of the restaurant, was too compelling to ignore. "I'm just gonna...I'll be right back," he said, standing. Fin nodded and waved as he walked quickly after Hayward.

In the narrow hallway at the back of the restaurant, the familiar thick scents of air freshener covered the smell of the restrooms, but also any of Hayward's scent. The flimsy wooden doors were both shut. He reached for the handle of the Males' just as the door cracked open and a golden eye peered out at him. "Coming?" Hayward sang softly.

A moment later, Amir was being shoved back against the locked door, Hayward's long muzzle licking at his shorter one, the black-furred paws sliding down his sides. Amir stiffened—in more ways than one—and

Hayward pulled back, straightening and looking down. "This okay?" he asked with a sparkle in his eye.

"Uh." Amir breathed in the red fox's scent, the closeness of him overwhelming the air freshener now, and nodded against his chest ruff. "Yeah, just...surprised me..."

"Good," Hayward said, and Amir wasn't sure what he meant by that, but he barely had time to wonder before an insistent muzzle was pressing back at his, warm breath along his whiskers and then over his cheekruff. Amir, not used to this kind of forwardness, but figuring it was only polite to take advantage of the implicit permission, wrapped his paws around Hayward's waist and pulled the slender fox closer to him. Hayward was excited too; he could feel that against his stomach even as his own arousal pressed against the red fox's thigh.

"Every fennec I've ever met," Hayward breathed, his lips just an inch from the soft fluff in Amir's ear, "likes his ears played with." He moved his nose up the inside of Amir's ear, breathing warmly and then, and then, just the barest tickle of a tongue along the fur.

Amir shuddered and closed his eyes, aware that his ear was trembling and that he was making some kind of soft squeaking sound, but unable to control any of it. "Mmm," Hayward breathed again, resting his muzzle against Amir's head with his nose just inside the cone of the ear, "I guess I have a trend."

His paw slid between them to cup Amir's sheath through the thin pants. "A definite trend," the red fox said, fingers rubbing agilely up the hard ridge.

Oh God, Amir thought, I'm going to get jerked off in a public bathroom again. He whimpered, but the only thing he could make himself do was to drop his paws to Hayward's rear, cupping and squeezing it and dimly registering through the haze of ear and sheath fondling that it was just as tight and perfect to touch as it was to look at, that the jeans were soft and supple, and that the muscles beneath them were anything but.

Hayward tensed his thighs at Amir's touch, grinding his body into the smaller fennec's. His muzzle kept playing along Amir's right ear, now giving bolder licks down into the depths of the ear that turned Amir's grasp on the fox's rear into desperate clutches just to keep himself upright. He squeaked louder, into a moan.

With a little tongue-flick, Hayward pulled his muzzle back. He looked down, golden eyes glinting, and teased Amir's sheath with a small dance of his fingers before removing that, too. "Maybe we should move this somewhere more private."

"Ah. Huh." Amir forced himself to nod, bracing himself against the thin wooden door until his legs recovered some strength. Now that his ears weren't full of tongue, he became aware of other sounds, people moving in the hallway outside.

"You ready to go back?"

Amir glanced down. He swallowed. "Maybe...a minute."

"You got it." Hayward touched Amir's nose with his finger and went over to the sink. He ran the water. "Need to use the...?" He jerked his head toward the urinal.

It would help if he did. Might make him presentable sooner. "Nah," Amir said, trying to think about the least sexy things he could. It didn't help to have Hayward's rear and tail waving in front of him. At least the person outside was courteous enough not to try the door. Perversely, the proximity just made him more excited.

Hayward turned around. "Ready yet?" He glanced down and grinned. "Okay, time for plan B, then. Stay behind me, 'kay?"

They strolled out of the bathroom together, Hayward in front, his bushy tail up against Amir's crotch. From behind the other fox, Amir had a great view not only of the wide-eyed expression of the lion in the narrow hallway, but also of Hayward's saucy smirk that made the lion narrow his eyes as he pushed past them into the small rest room.

At the table, Amir scooted into his chair. Fortunately, Fin had gotten his baklava and didn't look up until Amir was safely seated, a napkin over his lap. "Hopefully the date isn't over," the swift fox said after swallowing.

Folding his ears down over a hot flushing sensation was becoming more and more familiar for Amir. Hayward grinned, unfazed. "Oh, it's just getting started," he said. "I was thinking we should head off from here."

Fin scooped the last of the baklava onto his fork and into his muzzle. Amir nodded at it. "Walnuts?"

"Mm." Fin nodded.

"So," Hayward said across the table to Fin, "your place okay?"

Amir stared at him. Then Fin said, "Sure," and Amir stared at *him*.

"Don't be so worried," Hayward said to him, putting a paw on his knee under the table. "If you want to just go home, you can."

Maybe Fin had a spare room. Maybe Hayward just meant that they would go to Fin's place and Fin would go somewhere else. As weird as that sounded, nothing would surprise Amir anymore. And what else would he do? He was rock-hard, still, from being with Hayward in the bathroom, and his right ear was cool with the dampness of a tongue whose touch still tingled in his memory. He could always go home to his frigid apartment and jerk off. "No, I'm okay."

H

Fin's apartment, a short drive away, had real ceiling lights and a gleaming white kitchen, and it smelled like fresh-baked bread. It was a bit chilly, but nothing like Amir's place. The swift fox took their coats and hung them up in the closet while Hayward took Amir's paw and pulled him to the long futon-couch in front of the TV. "What's on TiVo?" Hayward called across the living room, already thumbing the remote.

"Does it matter?" Fin called back.

"What do you watch?" Hayward asked Amir as the screen came up.

Amir had the sense of being part of a play where nobody had given him a script. "I don't really watch a lot of TV," he said. "Mostly, like, CSI or Law and Order."

"Cops'n'courts," Fin said from the kitchen. "I don't record 'em, because there's always one on. You guys want a drink? Amir, you like wine?"

"Open that zin you got the other day," Hayward called.

"Sure, I like wine. Zin's great." Amir watched the shows go by on TiVo, and then his concentration was jolted slightly when Hayward rested a paw on his thigh. "I like, ah, Bearly Brothers too."

Fin said something about the writer of that show having come over from Mousetrap, which Amir only vaguely heard, because Hayward was teasing his fingers all along the inside of his thigh. "Sounds good to me," Hayward said, right into Amir's left ear.

Amir tensed up, especially when Fin came over. The dusk-colored fox stared down at them for a moment, a glass of wine in each paw, but just as Amir's hot self-consciousness was about to boil over, Fin set both glasses on the coffee table in front of them. "That's a good episode," he said, plopping down into the corner of the couch on the other side of Hayward. "Or you could just put on the music channel."

"I like to have things going on," Hayward said, starting the show and sliding his paw up to Amir's stomach.

The fennec shivered, not sure what to do, but Fin didn't seem to mind. Maybe he'd...go in the other room when things got further? He couldn't just sit there and let Hayward do all the groping, or the red fox would think he wasn't interested, so he dropped his paw on Hayward's muscular thigh and ran it up and down.

Hayward grinned and leaned toward him again. The fennec's large left ear had only a moment to twitch in anticipation before Hayward had pinned it to the couch, nuzzling it much as he had the other in the bathroom. He brushed the short fur of his muzzle along the inside, his breath warm against the fur, then progressed to short licks of his tongue, all the while leaning further over so that eventually, Amir's paw was forced away from his thigh and up to his fluffy white chest.

Amir ended up curled back into the corner of the futon, the armrest pressed against his tail and back, trying not to make squeaky whimpers as Hayward started licking further into his ear. It would probably be rude to start getting all...getting all...his paw gripped Hayward's chest and side, almost pulling the other fox onto him, the licking around his ear sending tingles all through him—no, not tingles, that would be like calling Lake Kasamee a puddle. They were more like electric currents. He loved having his ears licked, but God, what Hayward was doing was in a whole different league, the fox's tongue flicking switch after switch connected directly to his sheath.

Fin, completely blocked from Amir's view by Hayward's chest, chuckled softly. Amir had momentarily forgotten whose apartment he was in, the scent of the swift fox having faded to a background odor behind Hayward's strong scent right in his nose. "Oh," he panted, twisting his head slightly. "Should, uh..."

Hayward stopped in his licking, pulling his head back. He was now almost on all fours on the couch, facing Amir with a smile. "Don't worry. Fin's got plenty to occupy him."

Amir had meant to ask whether they should move to a room, or something else that would involve not making out in the same room as their host, but he took Hayward's assurance at face value. Apparently Fin was okay watching sitcoms while a couple friends—acquaintances, at least—groped and teased each other next to him, and rubbed their paws into their sheaths, as Hayward had now started to do. "Okay," he panted, angling his hips into the red fox's fingers.

"Good," Hayward said, and brought those fingers up. Almost before the fennec could say anything, his pants were open and slender fingers were diving inside, pausing only briefly at his boxers before finding the opening and pulling his shaft through it.

Amir just gave a little squeak. That first contact, someone else's fingers right there on your cock, always made him shiver and think about what was ahead. This time, what he mostly thought was whether Fin were watching, but he still couldn't see what the swift fox was doing. All he could see was the edge of the couch and the floor, where Fin's feet had been resting but were no longer. He squirmed around, rubbing his paw down Hayward's exposed stomach, trying to ignore all the social conventions he'd spent twenty-three years learning, that said that you don't pull out your cock in the apartment of someone you've just met unless he's the one pulling it out. At least, he thought, he needed to give Hayward something back. (And then he wouldn't be the only one exposed.)

But his short arms couldn't quite reach all the way. He squirmed down a bit, pushing his fingers through the soft white fur over Hayward's tight stomach, while the red fox's fingerpads teased up and up his shaft. He got his paw further down, expecting any moment to encounter soft denim, but there was nothing but fur. And then, abruptly, fingers.

For a flash, he thought Hayward was pawing himself. But the black fingers stroking Amir's erection were Hayward's, and the red fox was supporting himself with the other arm, his open vest hanging down. Amir looked up into sparkling golden eyes. "I told you Fin had something to occupy him," the fox said.

Fin's fingers brushed Amir's, and then grasped them gently and pulled them forward, wrapping them around a large, thick shaft. "Here," the deep voice rumbled, "if you'd like to hold on to this for a minute..."

Amir wrapped his fingers around it and saw Hayward's smile curve wider, the tip of his tongue protruding from between his lips. "Big," Amir murmured, circling it and then teasing up and down. It was warm, too, very warm. The tip was already dripping, letting Amir slicken it with each stroke.

"That's why I don't top," Hayward said, winking, his muzzle hanging open.

"Oh, is *that* why?" Fin said from behind him.

"Mmf." Hayward's eyes closed, then opened to look down at Amir with a wink. "There may be...other reasons."

Over his shoulder, Amir saw Fin's dusty grey muzzle come into view. The swift fox's paw, slick with something else, touched his again. "Other reasons, he says," he grinned. "Just one big reason, I says." Hayward's eyes narrowed and unfocused, his paw coming to rest on Amir's shaft, his whole body tight. Fin's eyes flicked downward. "And here it comes."

Amir watched, fascinated. He could see everything in Hayward's expression: the slight upward jerk of his muzzle at the touch under his tail, the bracing, clenched teeth in the wide smile, and then the lifted muzzle, jaw dropping to let the tongue loll out. When he let out a soft whine through his nostrils, a long, slow, happy sound, Amir thought it was like hearing the slide of Fin's cock into the other fox. He got a big smile on his own face, and felt his tail wag against the couch.

It was oddly reassuring to know that Fin was part of this and not just an awkward spectator, overwhelming Amir's own awkwardness. He'd always thought if he ever did participate in a threesome, it would be with two good friends, or a boyfriend and an ex, and they would talk about it beforehand. He hadn't ever figured he would get roped into one without knowing it. Nor that he would be okay with it so quickly. But Hayward's calm confidence was contagious.

Also, it was pretty easy to be okay with things when you were getting a nice handjob—a better than nice handjob, now that Hayward was stroking again, his body swaying in time with Fin's thrusts. And then Hayward lifted his paw. He grinned down, his eyes still slightly unfocused as his body bumped back and forth. "That's...reason number one," he panted, "and now...reason number two..."

He pushed Amir away along the couch, forcing the fennec's paw off his cock. Before Amir could protest, Hayward's head had dipped between his legs. "Ohh," he panted, and leaned back as the red fox lapped at his stiffness. A moment later, Hayward's lips parted and took Amir into his muzzle, all the way in.

The couch trembled in time with Fin's thrusts, Hayward's muzzle slurping down and up in the same rhythm. Amir's tail was too light to make much noise, but it wagged erratically as his body shivered, one paw coming to rest on Hayward's nicely muscled arm, the other gripping the fabric of the couch. He caught Fin's eye; the swift fox thrust forward, biting his lip, but when he saw Amir looking at him, he gave him a grin and a raised eyebrow.

That right there was a moment. That Fin could stop, even balls-deep in the red fox, and make sure Amir was okay—that was special. Most other times he'd gone right from "nice to meet you" to "get your pants off," they both just went at it, and felt awkward after. Amir had the feeling that Fin wouldn't normally be a one-night-stand kind of fox, and even though he himself was, out of necessity, he liked the idea that Fin wouldn't be. Feeling more at ease, he grinned back, and Fin winked at him.

Then Hayward leaned against the couch back for support, and reached up to brush fingers along Amir's ears, and the fennec just closed his eyes and let the sensations wash through him, no longer trying to restrain his squeaks of pleasure. Neither of the other foxes was making a noise—well, Hayward had his muzzle otherwise occupied, and Fin was panting heavily, which kind of counted. Any self-consciousness that remained about his squeaks vanished as Hayward's tongue slid along the hot length of his shaft, the sparks and shivers from that meeting the waves of delight from the caresses of his ears somewhere around his throat, generating louder and louder noises.

His paws clutched more tightly at Hayward and at the couch as his feet kicked, his body tensing. Hayward's tongue washed up, his lips sliding around, and Amir's shaft trembled under the attention. It had been months since anyone had had him in their muzzle, weeks since anyone'd even pawed him off, and the excitement pushed him faster and faster toward a climax. He wanted to ask Hayward if it was okay to come in his muzzle, because he didn't think he had much time to stop at this point, but his throat wasn't really available for words, so he just squeezed the red fox's arm and put more urgency into his squeaking moans.

Hayward didn't break his rhythm, though he did respond with a couple deep moans of his own, their vibrations reverberating through Amir's erection and sac. Amir took that as permission and let himself go, the licking pushing him over the edge. He arched his back, hips thrusting up into Hayward's muzzle, moaning in his climax. He felt himself spurting onto the red fox's tongue, felt Hayward's lips tighten around him and suck harder, and the world spun dizzily around for that time until Amir settled back to earth, panting happily, scrunched up in a corner of the couch.

"Mmm." Hayward kept his head down, his muzzle still locked around Amir's shaft, and now Amir had a better view of the red fox's tail swept to one side, Fin with one paw on Hayward's side and the other arm working hard out of sight, below the russet-furred back. The swift fox was leaning over now, his muzzle just a few feet from Amir's, eyes closed, still biting his lip, his moans coming faster. He forced a moan out through his nose, then another, louder, and then he slammed Hayward's body forward, almost on top of Amir.

Amir held Hayward's arm as Fin kept thrusting forward, a series of hard motions, and then let out a long breath, trembling just a little. His arm kept working, as Hayward's arm slid from Amir's ear down to his shoulder, holding him in return. The red fox's eyes closed, his breath warm on Amir's stomach, tongue gently flicking against the fennec's trapped shaft as Hayward rocked back and forth with his own motion for the first time.

When Hayward came, it was just as obvious as when Fin had first entered him. His body bucked and shuddered, though he kept his head perfectly still, and his breaths came hot and fast into Amir's fur. The already-sharp scent of musk grew stronger, and then Hayward lifted his head and smiled a dreamy smile, his eyes rapt, as though there were some gorgeous person just over Amir's shoulder. The look gave Amir a small shiver, and then Hayward's eyes focused on the fennec. He licked his lips, his nostrils flaring as though smelling Amir for the first time. "You're sweet," he said softly.

Amir giggled, warm with his climax still, only his shaft chilly and wet now that it was exposed. Hayward opened his muzzle to say something else, but then he stiffened and his ears flicked up. Behind him, Fin was removing his paw and scooting backwards. "Oh," Hayward sighed, "they feel almost as good going out as going in. You think?"

"Uh, I guess." Amir looked away at the TV, which was still showing whatever they'd put on twenty minutes ago.

"Aw, sweetie, we're all hanging out together." Hayward brushed the edge of Amir's ear. "No need to be embarrassed."

The glow of climax was fading, leaving behind the awkward reality of sitting on the couch half-naked with two guys he barely knew, the smell of come thick in the air. But if Amir pulled his pants up right away, that might make them feel awkward, too. He'd rarely been with anyone who wanted to hang out after sex. Usually it was uncomfortable good-byes, or rolling over to go to sleep. He nodded to Hayward and willed himself to relax.

"I'm gonna clean up," Fin said, getting up. "Be right back."

Amir couldn't help looking when the swift fox got up. He saw with some relief that the swift fox's glistening shaft was about the same size as his. So not everyone in Gateway was amazingly hung. A flash of wondering what that shaft would feel like under his tail passed quickly, with a small tingle.

Hayward settled onto the couch again, his own impressive erection still mostly out. "Sorry," he said, scooting next to Amir, "but it's a little wet over there."

"It's okay," Amir said.

Hayward put a paw on his knee. "I know this is a bit weird," he said. "But trust me. Fin's a really good guy."

"I like him." Amir squirmed away from Hayward. This wasn't how one-night-stands were supposed to end.

Lion Christ, he thought to himself, loosen up. This was what he'd wanted, wasn't it? Just because he wouldn't have thought he'd start with sex and then move on to the getting-to-know-them was no reason for him not to take advantage of the opportunity. So it felt weird—so what? It was weird, this whole situation. But hell, picking up guys in bars wasn't weird, and that didn't work at all. He thought about Fin's look, the raised eyebrow. Maybe it was time to give weird a try.

He sighed and settled against the red fox, and felt the tremor of his tail wagging. "I knew you would," Hayward said. He picked up his wine glass and took a deep drink. "You guys hit it off at dinner."

"I guess." Amir squinted at him. "You *were* asking *me* out, right?"

Red foxes could do sly grins like nobody else. Hayward said, "Of course, dear. But I have a lot of friends, and as Fin pointed out, two is better than one."

"But three is not better than two," Fin said, coming back with a towel in his paw. He'd taken his pants completely off, though he had pulled his boxers up. Amir could still see the outline of his sheath through them, and a damp spot where he was still leaking.

"Nowhere to put the third," Hayward agreed, putting down the wine and scooting closer to Amir as Fin wiped up the couch. He gave the fennec a peck on the muzzle and got up. "I'm gonna clean up myself. Want me to take that in to the bathroom?"

He held out his paw. Fin nodded and dropped the towel into it, then plopped himself down at the other end of the couch. "So," he said, "your first 'Hay Date.' What'd ya think?"

Now Amir pulled his pants up, tucking his damp shaft away. "Oh, it was fun," he said.

"God, the first time he did that to me, I wanted to slap him."

Amir looked at Fin, eyes wide. The swift fox was facing the TV, though his ears were cupped toward the fennec. "You've done this before?"

"A few times. Whenever Hay thinks he's met someone I'll like."

"Oh." Amir glanced at the damp spot on the couch. "Were you ever in the middle?"

Fin laughed, shortly. "You think Hay would let someone else take center stage?"

Amir grinned. "You've never done this without him?"

"I wouldn't know how. Hayward's...special." He smoothed his whiskers back, still seeming to watch TV. "If you want to do it without him, it won't be with me."

"Oh, no!" Amir flattened his ears back. "I just...one-on-one's enough for me. This was fun, but..."

"Not all the time. I'm with ya." Fin gave Amir a quick glance.

Amir nodded. He glanced back toward the bathroom, but the door was still closed. "It was weird...hey, thanks for checking on me."

Fin tilted his muzzle, then gave him a 'no problem' wave. "Hay can be a bit pushy. I wanted to make sure you were okay before we got everything all sticky."

"Yeah, it just all happened so fast. But it was fun," Amir said again.

"Hay's pretty good at checking people out before he brings 'em into this." Fin jerked his head back toward the bathroom. "If you'd freaked out about getting felt up in the bathroom at the restaurant, he wouldn't have brought you back here."

Amir's ears flushed. He dipped his muzzle. "What if we hadn't gotten along at dinner?"

"Same thing." Fin shrugged. "He likes his three-ways, but he likes to keep his friends, too."

Somehow, that put the whole weird episode into perspective. The awkwardness retreated, leaving him just sitting on a couch with a new acquaintance, talking about a mutual friend. "That's good to know."

"Oh, all dressed already." Hayward put on a mock pout, coming back from the bathroom. "Such a pity. Listen, boys, there's this terrific party starting, um, let me see, an hour ago. Shim's going to be there," he said to Fin, "and there'll be dancing and karaoke. What do you say?"

Amir hesitated. Fin chuckled. "I think I've had enough fun for one night."

"Okay." Hayward held his paw out to Amir. "Want to come with me? Or I can drop you off at home. Or you can stay here with Fin."

Amir glanced at Fin, and smiled. "Shouldn't Fin offer that?"

Hayward showed no signs of embarrassment. "Oh, he doesn't mind. I mean, look what we just did on his couch. He's a good host."

"If it's okay," Amir said, looking at Fin, "I wouldn't mind sticking around a bit. My apartment's not really..."

"Close?"

"Heated."

Fin smiled. "Gotcha. Sure, if you want. I've got some movies and microwave popcorn."

"Sounds awesome."

Hayward rolled his eyes. "Sounds boring. But you boys enjoy. I'll catch up with you at the bookstore," he said to Amir, and then turned to Fin. "And you...whenever."

"Thanks for the date," Amir said, getting up to shake paws, but Hayward pulled him into a hug.

"Anytime. You're fun. And loud." When Amir folded his burning ears down, Hayward kissed his nose. "Oh, silly. You should hear me when I don't have my muzzle full. It's epic."

He let go and crossed to Fin, who just brushed muzzles, and then Hayward was gone, with a bounce and a wave and a jaunty wag of his tail.

"Whew." Fin yawned, and started to pick up the wine glasses. Amir apologized for not having touched his, but Fin didn't seem to mind. "I always feel drained after an evening with Hay, and it's not even ten. Movies are over there if you want to pick one while I make popcorn."

Amir dropped to his knees to look through the stack, while Fin walked to the kitchen. From there, the swift fox called, "Uh, do you want, um, tea or something? I usually make a chai for myself. I've got Earl Grey, Orange Pekoe...coffee or pop, too, if you want."

"Chai's great." Amir pored over the collection, tail wagging, but he didn't think it mattered what they watched. As weird as it had been, he was sure he'd never have met Fin if not for Hayward. And Hayward was a character, definitely a strange fellow, probably not boyfriend material (though part of Amir wondered what it would be like to slide under that tail, or even to have that big cock work inside him). But Fin here was a quiet fox, who liked movies and books and chai, who was a little embarrassed at what they'd gone through, and whom Amir had already seen naked.

It wasn't a relationship, but, Amir thought, it was a better start than he'd had in years. He'd be sleeping alone tonight, almost for sure (almost), but he'd for darn sure get Fin's number. From Fin's movies, he selected

'Company'--perhaps a bit obvious, but it was what was on his mind. Besides, back in Viyajo, he'd been the only one who liked it. It was nice to think that here, he wasn't alone any more.

There were only three people Fin would interrupt a conversation to take a phone call from, and Hayward was the only one he wasn't related to. It was no knock on any of his other friends; if they established a history of getting him laid, he'd start taking their calls at any time too. He happened to be talking to the director of his local community theater about the rehearsal times for the coming week when his phone chimed with the "Three's Company" theme.

The director, a skinny pine marten, stopped in the middle of an animated sentence to raise an eyebrow. "Sorry," Fin said. "I need to take this." And he did, too.

At times, Fin felt as though he were living on an island, with tenuous drawbridges connecting him to the mainland, or to other people's islands. The director was being so insistent on specific rehearsal times that Fin was starting to get the "drawbridge up" feeling. Another five or ten minutes and he might've been cut off from the director and possibly the play.

The swift fox barely glanced at the name "Hayward" as he flipped his phone open, trotting down from the stage and partway up one of the aisles. "Hey, Hay," he said.

"Hey yourself." He could almost see the red fox's grin on the other end. "Busy tonight?"

"Oh, you know me. A hot date with Mr. DVD Collection."

"Can you stand him up?"

He grinned, brushing his paw along the seats, walking further up the aisle to make sure he was out of earshot of anyone on stage. Already he could feel his drawbridges lowering again, his chest relaxing. "Who's the dinner guest?"

"This adorable little fennec. He's new in town, he loves the theater."

"The theater, eh?" His tail swished. He turned to look down at the stage, where the director was engaging the lead actress, a buxom rabbit who was a capable enough singer, if not much else. "Like that raccoon who 'loved books'?"

"What about him?"

"He loved comics."

"Comic *books*, darling. Amir is much nicer. You'll like him. I guarantee it."

The director was trying to catch his eye. Fin held up one finger. "Or my money back?"

Hayward purred. "Have I ever let you down?"

Fin had to adjust his now-warm pants as he walked back to the stage. Hayward was a character, no doubt about that. Fin sometimes wondered if he spent all his time getting into threesomes. In the year and change since Hayward had picked him up outside a community theater last summer, he'd gone on six—no, seven—"Hay dates." He wasn't complaining, not by any stretch of the imagination, even if the threesomes were something he'd never ever do with anyone else. They were a Hayward thing, and Fin had long since stopped looking that particular gift horse in the mouth. Under the tail was much more fun.

Fin's winter coat had come in, keeping him warm enough that his overcoat was all he needed over his shirt and jeans. He'd grabbed the first collared shirt he'd come across, knowing it didn't really matter much what he wore.

He and Hay had been to the Ankara Café enough that even though it was under new management since their last visit, the hostess recognized him. "Evening, sir," the deer said with a smile. "You're with the gentlefox in the red vest, yes?"

"Yes." Fin smiled. "Thank you."

She led him to where Hayward was typing on his smartphone, at a small table for three against one wall of the restaurant. The red fox smiled brightly and stood, tucking his phone into his vest pocket and reaching out to hug Fin. Their muzzles brushed, giving Fin a powerful reminder of his scent. It always amazed him that Hayward didn't use any artificial perfumes; his musk reminded Fin of a damp cedar forest, strong and delightful without being overpowering.

"How's the play going?" Hayward asked as they sat.

Fin sighed. "It *looks* good. If only Charisse could act."

"When are you going to play a lead?"

"When I get a new job with flexible hours." Fin took the water glass as soon as the waiter put it down.

Hayward lifted a paw. "There'll be one more joining us. Can I have a glass of the cab?"

"Same here," Fin said. When the waiter'd left, he looked into Hayward's grin and shook his head. "So where did you meet this one?"

"At the Foxed Page. He was there almost every day for the past two weeks." Hayward set his elbows on the table, laced his fingers together, and rested his muzzle on them. "Curled up in the couch, so cute with those big ears."

"Which means you were there every day for two weeks," Fin said. "Taking up reading?"

Hayward smiled. "It's on my way home from work."

"Of course it is." Fin nodded. "So is the lingerie store."

"Are you into cross-dressing? I've heard that about you theater types." Fin started to say something, but Hayward leaned back and held up a paw. "Hold on, I'm trying to imagine you in a dress. Something sheer, something in a...hm, I think a nice ocher sundress would offset your fur nicely."

"Thank you," Fin said as drily as he could.

"Of course, you can't go wrong with orange." Hayward brushed imaginary dust from the russet fur on his arm.

"You told this guy it's just a casual date, right?"

"I'm pretty sure he knows that."

Fin frowned. "You told him you were meeting me, right?"

"Well, I didn't mention you specifically." Hayward smiled. "They still have the lamb here. Good."

Fin leaned across the table. "Listen, Hay, I don't want to give this guy the wrong idea, that this might lead to something."

Hayward spread his paws. "What wrong idea? He doesn't even know you're going to be here."

Fin rolled his eyes. "I really wish you wouldn't—" He stopped as the waiter returned with their wine, asked if they were still waiting for one, and left when Hayward nodded.

"Mm." Hayward took a sip. "The whites here aren't very good, but they do have a nice cab."

Fin left his wine on the table. "Why didn't you tell him?"

Hayward lowered his glass. "You have to trust me. How many times have you done this?"

"That's not the point. The point is—"

"Oh, there he is." Hayward half-stood. "Amir!"

Fin turned to see a fennec stopped by the hostess's stand, looking at them with a familiar expression of dismay and confusion. He shook his head. "Oh, Hayward."

"Just relax," Hayward said with a smile as the fennec approached. He introduced Fin and Amir to each other, giving them a chance to examine each other while he asked Amir if he wanted wine.

"Whatever you're having," the fennec said. Fin sipped his wine, taking a good look. The guy was presentable enough. He knew how to dress, and his scent was pleasant, very dry, but spicy as well, like a pepper plant. He had a nice voice, a little higher than Hayward's, and a bit of a drawl. Not much, not the thick mauling of vowels you'd get in the south, just a little spicy, like his scent. Fin liked the sound of it, and he had to admit that Hayward was right: those huge ears were adorable. Also, he had the good taste to accept Fin's recommendation for the orange chicken stew dinner.

It turned out that Amir was from a town near Chevali called Viyajo, which explained the accent. Moving from the southwestern desert up to the northern Midwest was quite a change, and it made Fin curious. "So what brings you to Gateway?" he asked.

Amir held his paws in front of his on the table and didn't quite look at Fin, though he wasn't looking at Hayward, either. "City planning."

"Ah, Pinewood's good for that. I have a friend who went there. He's an architect now, works downtown. Actually, he was in that production of *Much Ado*, too," he told Hayward. "Set design."

"Are you still involved with the theater?" Amir asked him.

Fin perked his ears. Maybe the fennec really was interested in plays. "I'm in the next production at the Rosewood Stage and Sound. We're putting on *Picnic*." Amir nodded, showing no sign of recognition. "By William Inge."

Amir just nodded and said, "Ah," his eyebrows furrowing slightly.

If he'd been into plays, he would've recognized Inge's name, no question. Fin shot Hayward a look, but the red fox was pointedly ignoring him, looking at Amir. "I've no idea who that is," he said, "but Fin is always in the most interesting plays."

"What's it about?" Amir asked.

"Sex and love in a small town." Fin shrugged. "Two sisters, falling in love with the wrong guys. It won a Pulitzer. Our director's turned it into a musical."

Hayward clapped his paws together, but Amir frowned. "Well, I hope it's good," he said. "I'm all for musicals, but if it won a Pulitzer..." Fin raised an eyebrow. Amir's expression changed, his ears sliding back. "I mean, I'm sure it's good, if you're...if you like it."

"It's not all bad." Fin smiled. "I get to sing a duet in one song."

"He's going to be playing the lead before long," Hayward said.

"There's no one lead in this one," Fin said. "My character's pretty important."

"I'd like to see it," Amir said, and he sounded honest.

Fin smiled. "You go to many plays?"

"There wasn't much theater in Viyajo," Amir said. "My mom took me to Chevali once to see *Beauty and the Beast*."

Fin tried to keep his expression polite, but he needn't have bothered. "It would've been more fun if I'd been twelve," Amir said, grinning. "I went up again last year with some friends and we ended up getting tickets to *Wicked* when it was on tour. Now that was awesome. Except for the one guy who was totally drunk in front of us. He kept singing along to the songs."

"I wish people would care enough about our plays to sing along with the songs," Fin said. "And you haven't seen a real spectacle 'til you've seen one of the actors drunk."

"Does it happen a lot?" Amir asked.

Fin nodded, but before he could say anything, Hayward grinned. "He's had an incident or two of his own."

"I was not drunk," Fin said.

"You were under the influence."

"I didn't have any lines," he told Amir, who was smiling. "I just had to walk out and be part of a crowd."

"And he got distracted and just kept walking," Hayward said.

Amir giggled. "Really?"

"It played fine." Fin folded his arms. "Michel even said so."

"He'd have said anything when you had his cock in your mouth." Hayward grinned slyly at him.

"That had nothing to do with it," Fin said. Of course Hayward would have to bring that up. He glanced at Amir, but the fennec seemed more amused than anything else. He sighed. "He was always honest with me."

"Which is why you're not sucking his cock anymore."

"No." Before Hayward could reply, Fin turned to Amir. "Nobody really noticed, because that was during the week that the two leads broke up. So they were supposed to have all this romantic energy, and they could barely bring themselves to talk to each other."

"Oh God," Hayward said. "Tell him what the bitch did."

Fin leaned in and lowered his voice, thinking as he did that what he was going to say wasn't really any worse than Hayward's remark about his cock-sucking, which he'd cheerfully announced to the surrounding tables, but hell, he wasn't Hayward. "So there's this scene early on where the guy makes a move on the girl and she fights him off. This was the night after she found out he was cheating on her, and they'd spent the afternoon having a screaming fight, and she didn't want to go on, but her understudy had a bad cold, so she had to. Anyway, he makes his move, and there was some line, I forget what it was, about how pretty she is. Like, "You look so sweet and pure in the moonlight." And under his breath, when he says it—she told me this later—he says the name of the girl he was cheating with."

"Oh, shit," Amir said. "On purpose?"

Fin nodded. Hayward wagged a finger. "That still doesn't excuse what she did next."

Amir grinned. "What did she do?"

"Well, he puts his paw on her tit, and she's supposed to just push him away. But instead, she knees him in the balls."

Amir's smile vanished. "Oh, shit," he said again. "For real?"

Fin nodded. "He got his next two lines out and then his understudy had to finish the night."

Amir shook his head. "That's nuts."

Fin and Hayward both looked at him, grinning, and when he realized what he'd said, he started laughing. "I mean..."

"We know," Hayward said. "But that's not even the craziest thing Fin's seen." So then Fin had to tell the story about the guy who'd flashed the audience in the last scene of his last performance, which was a funnier story, if not as dramatic.

"There was a guy in my English class in college who was an actor," Amir said. "He always seemed just a little too into it. Like when he was studying *The Crucible*, he went and got all authentic period clothing and wouldn't wear anything else."

"Did he talk in period, too?" Fin asked.

"Forsooth." Amir grinned, and all three of them laughed. Hayward shot Fin a quick *What do you think?* look, but Fin didn't respond. They paused as the waiter returned with pita bread and some hummus, and then to sample it once he'd left.

"Are you at all interested in acting?" Fin asked, more to be polite than because he was expecting Amir to be, but the fennec nodded.

"I did a little in college, but I'd like to learn. I mean, it'd be fun to hang around and see a play get made."

"It's a lot of work." Fin finished off his wine. "The presidium arch is built on blood and tears." The quote earned him an eyeroll from Hayward, but Amir didn't seem to mind.

"Oh, I know. I worked on Habitat For The Homeless with a guy who built sets for plays. He said houses were easier 'cause you didn't have an art director changing his mind every three days about what the sets need to look like."

Fin laughed, and then leaned forward. "You built houses?"

"Mm." Amir swallowed the piece of pita he'd been chewing, and told them about the houses he'd built, and the family of kangaroo rats that had moved in.

Hayward gave Fin a look that said *So?* while his muzzle said, "I know the local Habitat guy. He's a possum, really lovely."

By the time the food arrived, Fin had decided that at the very least, Amir was interesting enough to spend the rest of the night with. So when Hayward gave him the fourth or fifth questioning look that evening, he gave a quick nod in response. The red fox smiled broadly and dug back into his chicken, engaging Amir in more questions about his Habitat work.

And when that talk flagged, Fin asked Hayward what he'd been up to lately, giving the fox a chance to tell them about the parties he'd been to and the latest drama at his office. "I swear," he said, when Hayward had wrapped up a story about one of his co-workers throwing a potted plant across the office upon hearing he'd been passed over for a promotion, "you have more drama in that one office than I've heard of from all the rest of my friends."

"The travel industry is full of colorful personalities," Hayward said with a wink.

The waiter arrived to clear their plates, and Fin knew that this was the point where Hay was going to take Amir back to see how game he was for the rest of the night. So he engaged the waiter in conversation about the baklava, asking how they made it, something pointless that would let Hayward nudge Amir toward the back bathroom. Sure enough, the red fox excused himself, and the fennec left a moment later, stammering uncertainly. Fin gave him a careless wave. Poor thing probably still thought he was just on a date with Hayward.

He ordered the baklava and then sat back. Though he knew it was part of Hayward's plan, part of him still felt left out, left alone. He fought the feelings, both the annoyance and the relief, and quoted Pope to himself, one of his favorite lines: "On life's vast ocean diversely we sail."

His eyes and ears flicked to the back hallway, as though he could see or hear what Hayward was doing to Amir back there. His sheath stirred enough for him to adjust it with a paw. If Amir wasn't willing, Hayward would bail on the date, but the fennec seemed friendly enough. Fin wasn't as good a judge of people as Hayward was, but he figured Amir would be game. And if not, maybe he and Hayward could get each other off.

The baklava arrived, and Fin had made his way through two bites of the sweet, flaky pastry when Hayward sauntered back across the room, Amir close behind him. It didn't matter that the fennec was obviously trying to hide his groin; Fin could see Amir's arousal in Hayward's smugly satisfied expression. And, a moment later, in the fennec's slacks, as he slipped out of the cover of the red tail and sat quickly.

"Hopefully the date isn't over," he said, pretending not to have noticed, and the red fox grinned at him.

Of course they went back to his place. Hayward wouldn't ask Amir to host, and they couldn't go to Hayward's for reasons Fin had never fully determined. With the money the red fox spent on clothes and parties, it was possible he lived in a little shithole studio off the river. Fin had never asked, and Hayward had never volunteered. But that meant Fin had expected that and tidied up, though when they walked in the front door, he realized he'd forgotten to put a cover on the sofa. He went to the closet to get one, but Hayward had already installed himself and Amir there by the time Fin could do anything about it.

He didn't want to make a big deal out of it, even though he felt a reflexive twinge of annoyance at the intrusion. Sure, he'd invited them in, but Hayward had this habit of making himself at home that sometimes grated. Just a bit, not enough for Fin to stop talking to him or stop inviting him over; in fact, he always forgot about it until the next time. And then he would have to suppress that annoyance all over again. It wouldn't be so bad if it were just the two of them, but Hayward's focus on Amir gave Fin the sense of being an outsider again, more galling since it was in his own apartment.

Intellectually, though, he knew it was silly, and besides, he was pretty sure he'd be fucking Hayward before too long, which would make up for all of it, so rather than say anything or go to the trouble of pouting, he just offered them drinks. And of course Hayward remembered the zinfandel. That fox had a memory for wine that Fin envied. Of course, he had a pretty good memory for everything. The zin was the perfect wine for the occasion: piquant and flavorful, but not so expensive that it would be a waste if, as Fin suspected, it ended up sitting on the coffee table untouched.

Sure enough, Hayward's and Amir's glasses were still full when the red fox turned his attention to the fennec's ears. Judging from the panting and the occasional squeak, Amir liked that quite a bit. Fin let his paw trail down to his own sheath, enjoying the sounds and rubbing himself hard. Once Hayward started getting worked up, he'd be ready pretty quickly. Fin trailed his other paw through the red fox's tail, thinking about what lay beneath it.

It'd been three weeks since Hayward had called him, and in that time he'd not been with anyone but his paw. That explained the speed with which he got hard; sometimes it took him a good fifteen minutes, by himself. He waited to undo his pants until he heard a breathless, louder squeak from Amir, who certainly made some cute noises.

By this time, Hayward was up on all fours, tail hiked and legs spread. Fin reached up and brushed the tail softly, bringing it to his muzzle and nipping. It twitched in response, so he kept nipping and slid his paw between the inviting legs. There was the big hard shaft he remembered. He slid his fingers along it, as Hayward pushed his rear back into the rubbing. It smelled like he'd gotten the fennec's pants open, and just then Amir started to say something, and Hayward said, "Don't worry, Fin's got plenty to occupy him," pushing his sheath into Fin's paw as he did.

Fin grinned, giving Hayward's tail a good chew as his paw unfastened the red fox's pants and pulled them down his thighs, letting his sheath and member hang free and exposing that lovely, tight, red and white rear. One paw on his erection and one on Hayward's, he stroked evenly, closing his eyes and losing himself in the dual sensations.

Fingers brushed his. He opened his eyes and saw that Amir was squirming, no doubt trying to help out. Nice guy. While Hayward said something to him, Fin took his paw and wrapped it around Hayward's cock. "Here," he said, "if you'd like to hold onto this for a minute."

He reached down for the lube he kept under the couch and slathered his own cock in it, while Amir said something about how big Hayward was and Hayward said some nonsense about that being why he didn't top. "Oh, is that why?" he said, jamming a couple slick fingers into the fox's tailhole. There was no need to do that; the fox was relaxed and ready, but Fin liked it as part of the ritual.

"Mmf." Hayward's body trembled, clenching and then relaxing around Fin's fingers. "There may be...other reasons."

When he moved around into position behind Hayward, on his knees, his head was high enough to see Amir. The fennec looked like he was enjoying himself but was still a little apprehensive. Fin smiled, trying to put him at ease. "Other reasons, he says. Just one big reason, I says." He withdrew his paw and positioned himself at Hayward's slick tailhole. "And here it comes."

He shut out Amir for the moment and focused on the warmth squeezing his shaft as he pressed it forward into Hayward's shuddering hips. Fin held the red's narrow waist and nuzzled the tip of the twitching tail, pushing his hips further and sliding all the way in, closing his eyes. It was always good with Hay, more than most other bottoms he knew; the red had a way of pulling him in, of coming alive with a contagious energy that just made the whole thing better. Plus, he usually had his muzzle around someone else at the time, and that made the whole thing even more hot.

Which reminded Fin that it was Amir's first time. He opened his eyes and craned his head around, pulling his hips back slowly to let his cock feel Hayward's tightness, and he caught Amir's eye. The fennec looked a little apprehensive, but when he saw Fin looking at him, he smiled. Fin gave him a raised eyebrow "you okay?" and got a wider grin back. So he was cool. Fin winked at him and got back to the business of fucking Hayward.

And it was only a business in the sense that it took up most of his concentration. That red fluffy tail, spasming along against his muzzle, the muscular body under his paws, and the tailhole that clenched around him as he thrust in and slowly pulled back out engaged all his senses, leaving little room to focus on what was happening around him. Not to mention the thick, hard length he had to remember to stroke in his slick paw, thumb teasing that sensitive part Hayward liked.

All the while, he could feel his knot growing, pushing against Hayward's tailhole with each thrust. The familiar pressure at the base of his shaft held his passion in check, but not for much longer. He listened for the moans from Amir, watching Hayward's black ears bob faster and the slender tan body beyond them arch and shudder.

There was no question that Amir had come. Once he'd done moaning, he collapsed back, and Fin heard Hayward's "mmm," as he swallowed. By that time, he himself was pretty close, so he leaned further over the red fox, pressing the bushy red tail between them as his hips drove his shaft beneath it. He didn't neglect Hayward's shaft either, his paw working busily up and down, trying to time the trembling of their twin arousals to a common peak.

But Hayward had remarkable stamina, and had likely been fucked more recently than Fin had gotten off. The swift fox panted harshly, his arousal building up beyond what his knot could hold back. He wanted to jam it under the red fox's tail, to stick it there and feel the muscles squeeze the passion from him, but that he could restrain. His body's needs, no. They built up in his groin and spread to his chest, bringing short barking moans to his clenched teeth.

He felt the rush of his climax through the connection between him and Hayward, pumping out into the fox in shuddering waves. For a moment, he held still, his body singing with the peak, and it felt as though his spirit were going to escape his body. He thought, as he often did as he slipped from climax into afterglow, of the phrase "la petite mort," the little death, and how it felt to return slowly to life from it.

Because he couldn't just relax; he had a fox to finish. It didn't take long for him to get Hayward going; most likely the pressure of his knot and the thrusting of his body had pushed the fox close enough that it only took a few more strokes to get him over the edge.

And that was always nice, too, the rush of sticky warmth over his paw, the bucking below him, the shuddering that he'd so recently felt himself. He smiled and nibbled on one of the big black ears as he felt Hayward jerk in orgasm, wrapping both arms around the fox to hold him tightly, as much to give him the pleasure of being squeezed as to feel the rippling of the muscles as best he could. "Yeah," he whispered into the ear nearest his muzzle, "you come for me, you hot foxy you."

The flick of Hayward's tail told him he'd been heard, even though the red fox immediately slumped forward toward Amir. Fin felt a faint flutter of annoyance, but not enough to break through the warm post-orgasmic haze. Once the threesome was over, he always forgot that it was the new one who got all Hayward's attention. He slid backwards and pulled out, shivering at the sparks he felt at the light pop. His shaft bobbed there, his knot still pretty full, while Hayward murmured something to Amir, and the little fennec uncurled from the corner of the couch.

"I'm gonna clean up," Fin said, standing. "Be right back."

Neither of them really took notice. He padded quickly to his bathroom, taking down one of the spare washcloths and wiping first his paw, then his shaft. He took a breath and reached up to his medicine cabinet to get the small bottle of his antidepressants, and shook a pill into his paw. As he swallowed, he wondered whether Amir would leave with Hayward. The fennec seemed like more the quiet sort, and Hayward was trying to set up the two of them, after all. But he wasn't sure, now he thought of it, that he wanted Amir to stay. He was kind of tired, and he wanted to get some of his play reading in.

When he pulled his boxers up and went back out, Hayward went to clean up, leaving Fin to look at the mess on the center cushion of the sofa. Dammit. He apologized to Amir about it, not wanting the fennec to think him a slob. And to his surprise, out of nowhere, Amir said, "Hey, thanks for checking on me."

The remark got Fin's attention. Amir's whole caution about the situation had been cute. He didn't always "check up" on the new guys, but none of the ones he had had mentioned it after. It felt nice, being appreciated.

So the guy had manners, and liked one-on-one, and he had picked Fin's favorite episode of the Bearly Brothers to watch. So when Hayward came back and offered Amir the choice between going to a party with him and staying at Fin's place—without asking—Fin wasn't really upset when Amir said he'd rather stick around, play reading or not.

Hayward took off in that way he always did, leaving Fin feeling a little breathless and let down, rather like another "petite mort" itself. For a moment, he stood there awkwardly, looking at Amir. To occupy himself, he reached for Hayward's half-empty wine glass. "Oh," Amir said, taking a sip of his. "Sorry."

"It's okay." Fin picked up his own glass. "Movies are over there if you want to pick one while I make popcorn." He walked into the kitchen and had already picked up his chai before it occurred to him that he should offer some to Amir. "Uh, do you want, um, tea or something?"

He did. Chai, as it turned out. Interesting. But it didn't mean anything.

When he returned with tea and popcorn, Amir was holding out "Company." Fin suppressed a flicker of interest; picking the older musical that had been one of his favorites since he was a cub didn't mean anything, either. Probably.

He put the movie in and sat on one side of the couch, handing Amir his chai across the messy center cushion. "Give me a minute to throw this in the hamper," he said, and pulled the cushion out, taking the whole thing back to the bedroom as he stripped the cover off and dropped it in with his dirty clothes. He'd do laundry tomorrow.

When he came back to the living room, Amir was sipping his chai, curled up in a cute little ball on the cushion at the end of the couch. Fin

Bridges

took his chai and sat on the other, at the other end. They watched perhaps two minutes of the movie, and Fin was just settling into the rhythms of the actors on screen when Amir said, "So what's your deal?"

Fin looked away from the movie to the fennec, whose ears were pointed right at him. They could almost be in college again, a couple guys hanging out watching a movie late at night in their boxers, except that Fin's nights in college had never included a three-way, and had rarely ended with his cock in anything but his own paw. He felt the drawbridges begin to go up; who was this guy to be asking about him? But the memory of the noises he made when coming, the way he'd been so attentive at dinner, the little thank-you after sex, all that intimacy kept his bridges down. "I'm not seeing anyone," he said. "But that doesn't mean I don't like a little fun now and then."

"I figured." Amir had a cute semi-bashful grin. "But I mean, well, it sounds like you do a lot of social stuff, like the play and the book club and all, but you live alone...right?" He glanced at the door.

"Right," Fin laughed. "No roommate's gonna walk in on us. No, I like hanging out with people, but I like having my own space, you know what I mean?"

Amir inclined his head. "Guess so. Out in the desert, y'know, we had a big house and I always had plenty of room. Even when I went to the city, it's all spread out."

"Did you live in a dorm?"

The fennec shook his head. "Off campus. Commuter college."

Fin nodded. "I grew up on the prairie. Flat and big and just gorgeous. We could see for miles. *Ah, fields, beloved in vain, where once my careless childhood stray'd.*"

"Sounds great."

"I hated it."

Amir raised an eyebrow. Fin nodded and went on. "So boring. Nothing happened there. I love Gateway."

"I'm starting to like it too." Amir grinned. "So...how'd you get in with Hayward? He doesn't seem your type."

"I don't know if Hay's anybody's type." Fin rubbed his whiskers. "He just kind of takes people under his, um, wing."

Amir laughed at his hesitation. "So I noticed. Well, I'm glad he did. I'm not all that good at meeting new people." Fin didn't respond, and for a moment the two of them just watched "Company." Then Amir said, slowly, "What happened to the other guys?"

"Hm?" Fin looked over.

Amir had pulled his knees up and wrapped his arms around them. "You said Hayward's done this before, so...introduced you to other guys?"

"Oh. Yeah." Fin took a sip of chai to cover the flutter in his stomach. If not for the pills, he probably wouldn't be able to talk about his past relationships. But what had happened to them? Vecir, Mikka, and what was the name of the other one? Something that started with 'S.'

"If you don't want to talk about it, that's cool."

"Yeah, probably not." Fin inhaled the aroma of his tea, trying to remember that third name. It bothered him more that he'd forgotten that, though he could picture the black panther it belonged to, tall and a bit pudgy around the middle, but with no body-image problems; he'd gotten completely naked for Hayward, sprawled out on the couch. They'd traded phone numbers, but Fin had been out the first couple times he called. And he didn't call after that.

"This is kinda silly." Amir put down his chai and moved his cushion to the middle of the couch, then set himself on it again. "I mean, we were both just...pretty exposed to each other."

"Doesn't mean we know each other." But Fin smiled as he said it.

"I know." Amir sighed.

Fin was seized with the urge to reach out and put his arm over the fennec's shoulders. Don't do it, he told himself. It'll just lead to complications. "I love this song," he said instead, distracting them both with the movie.

Shaun, that had been his name. He'd taken off with Hayward after that first date. Mikka'd stuck around just as Amir was doing, and they had talked about, what, restaurants or something? They'd gotten together for dinner, but without Hayward, there hadn't been a spark, and Fin wasn't interested in forcing anything.

And would he be so unhappy if Amir faded off into the distance as well, just another anonymous cock on the other end of Hayward? He shifted his muzzle just slightly, so he could see the fennec, the short muzzle, the half-smile one gets while watching something that has just made you laugh or that you expect will make you laugh, the brightness in his eyes, and the twitching of his whiskers that showed that he was aware of Fin and his movements.

But for all that, Fin didn't really know him. And that was where Hayward's philosophy broke down. Just being naked in the same room with someone, even after talking to him through dinner, didn't mean things would stick. Shaun had been lively and chatty during dinner, too. So had Mikka.

On the other hand, neither of them had asked much about Fin and Hayward, sort of taking it for granted that they were being set up. And neither of them had the patience to sit next to Fin and watch a movie afterwards to decompress. He turned his muzzle a little more, seeing the reflection of the screen in Amir's brown eye.

Just then, Amir turned and looked at him, and smiled in a way that had nothing to do with the movie. Caught off guard, Fin smiled awkwardly and snapped forward to watch the movie again. He thought he heard a soft, amused snort, but his ears caught nothing after that.

And when the movie was done, Amir thanked him for the chai and the "hosting," and made sure to take down the address of the theater. "Like Hayward said," he said, standing at the door, "I'm at The Foxed Page most afternoons, up in one of the couches. So if you feel like dropping by, the café next door has a pretty good chai."

"Yeah, I like it," Fin said. He liked that Amir hadn't asked to exchange phone numbers. Leaning forward to brush muzzles, he was surprised by a quick kiss on his nose. When he drew back, Amir was smiling.

"I'd like it if you came by," the fennec said.

"I'll see you," Fin said. "At the theater or the store."

He watched Amir's fluffy tail bounce down the hall and then closed the door slowly. The scents of Amir, Hayward, and sex lingered, mingling with the chai and wine and popcorn, so he turned on the vents to clear out the air before turning out the lights. In the aftermath of a Hay Date, he was used to feeling physically happy and mentally ambivalent. It was interesting that Amir had managed to break that pattern, leaving him with the stirrings of real interest. Fin smiled to himself, lying staring at the ceiling. Was it possible that Hayward had finally gotten it right?

Most nights, he saw himself pulling the drawbridge up in his mind as he retreated into sleep, but this night, he left it down.

CHAPTER 3: NOVEMBER

The problem of Fin had nagged in the back of Hayward's mind for weeks, ever since the date with Vecir, which he'd been sure would work out. Part of him considered giving up, but the other part, the part he listened to more often the last few years, wouldn't let him. Not even during work.

"Of course," he said on the phone to the potential customer, "you *can* do all this yourself on the Internet. But we've been doing this for years. We know the best deals, and we know some of the out-of-the-way places that you might not."

No matter whom he brought over to the swift fox, nothing seemed to click. Not that the dates themselves weren't enjoyable; any time he could get a couple friends, or potential friends, off at the same time was a good night. But whenever he asked about the dates, Fin replied in vague, guarded tones that Hayward knew better than to question.

Which wouldn't be a problem if Fin seemed happy on his own. But he didn't, really. Hayward had seen the anti-depressants in his medicine cabinet. No matter how much he protested that he was fine, he always looked forward to meeting new people, and Hayward could just tell that Fin was looking for someone but was afraid to get close.

"Absolutely," he told the customer. "We have relationships with the biggest hotel chains and cruise lines. I can get you a better deal than I got the Mortensons, in fact, because the cruise they took is offering a discount this week only. Did I hear correctly that you are also otters?"

So a couple weeks ago, he'd started walking through a bookstore that was on his way home, The Foxed Page. Besides the tasteful name and nearly all-vulpine clientele, the bookstore was very conducive to sitting around and relaxing, so he scanned it for single foxes reading books who pinged his gaydar, and after a week, he'd zeroed in on one.

"I'm sure you'll love the Dynasty Cruise," he said into the phone. "I've never had an otter come back dissatisfied. The seafood is top-notch and the glacier sliding is an absolutely unique experience. Trust me on this."

There was this fennec, and the way he looked at Hayward's intentionally-tight pants left little doubt in Hayward's experienced mind what the guy was thinking (*"hot red fox"*). His tight pants and open shirt were tailored to create an impression, and he had become adept at catching looks in his peripheral vision, listening for suspended breath, all the signs that told him that impression had been successfully made.

"All right, then, I'll make all those arrangements for you. Would you like me to send you the tickets? We'd love to see you in person, if you can come by the office to pick them up. Then we can go over them together and make sure there's no mistake."

What he didn't know was whether the fennec would be interested in him, or in Fin, which meant that this afternoon, it would be time for phase two. He'd put on his tightest jeans, even though it meant he kept having to undo the top button whenever he sat down, and he had his fancy dark vest with the gold trim packed in his bag, so he could take his shirt off when he got to the bookstore.

"I'll look forward to seeing you then. Thanks so much, Mrs. Silverton. I know you won't be disappointed."

Not that his shirt was that bad, it was just not quite enough. In summer, he could've worn a nice short-sleeved silk, but in winter, alas, it had to be cotton, and cotton just did not wear as nicely. Better to go completely without. His fur was thicker in winter anyway.

Fortunately, even with his particular wardrobe, he didn't stand out in his office. Mella, the squirrel who sat at the next desk, wore garish red makeup on her eyebrows and had gold highlights in her cheekruffs; next to her was a lanky marten whose whole muzzle might have been magnetized for as many pieces of metal as he'd stuck through it.

Mella looked up as he got off the phone. "Was that *Regina* Silverton?"

"Could there be more than one?" Hayward chuckled.

"I don't know how you manage to stay so calm with her. She called me a hustler!"

"Sweetie," Hayward said, "you kinda are."

Mella snorted. "Like you're not."

"I'm just better at it." Hayward grinned, and she swatted his tail as he swished it toward her.

"Stop bragging, Hay," the marten called from his desk. "Some of us are trying to get through another depressing day of sending other people to paradise without being reminded of how inferior we are."

"Good luck with that," Hayward called over.

"Bitch," the marten muttered as he bent back to his papers.

"*Successful* bitch," Hayward corrected him, but he kept his voice low.

On his other side, a taller red fox looked up, adjusting his round glasses over the grey on his muzzle. "Careful, hon," he said. "Don't want to ruin another plant."

"We moved them out of his reach." Hayward stretched. "Is it five o'clock yet?"

"Ten 'til."

"Close enough." Hayward logged out of his terminal, stood, and fastened the top button of his pants. "Got things to do."

The marten looked at Hayward and then called over to a short badger, browsing a newspaper at his desk in the corner of the office. "Hey, Pete. If I suck your cock, can I leave early too?"

Pete lowered the newspaper and stared over his glasses at the marten. "When you make your numbers for fourteen straight months, then you can leave early." He raised the newspaper. "When you make them for twenty straight months, then you can suck my cock," he said from behind it.

Hayward, pulling his coat from the coat rack, laughed, and so did Mella and the others. The marten glared down at his desk. Pete, the only one who'd been there longer than Hayward's three and a half years, was one of the first people he'd set up, and he was still with Benjy. Since they'd adopted a cub, Hayward didn't see him outside of work much.

Hayward's phone chimed just as he was shrugging his overcoat over his shoulders. He picked it up and looked at the text message, from Vico: *Hay, when u gona cal me again?* In his mind, he could hear the nasal whine in the jaguar's voice, the one he hadn't noticed at first, largely because there hadn't been much talking at their first meeting. "What am I gonna do with him, Foster?" he murmured. The poor kid needed someone, but he needed someone strong and firm, like a father figure, and Hayward just didn't know anyone like that who wasn't already taken.

The smell of pine lingered faintly in his nostrils. Vico didn't need someone like Fin did, though. Vico was fine. Probably driving his mom and sister crazy, but he was fine. And Hayward knew what he needed; he just didn't know where to get it yet. Fin was more a question of getting closer and closer until he found someone who clicked. And maybe this fennec was the one.

Happily, when Hayward poked his nose up into the second story of The Foxed Page, the fennec was sitting in the corner of the couch there again. Hayward had dumped his coat and made sure to fluff up his chest and tail before he walked upstairs. He walked past the fennec, felt the guy's eyes on him, and made sure to slow down, to give him a good look.

He drank it in, all right, until Hayward glanced back and saw his nose dive back into his book, his ears a little pink.

God, he was adorable. Hayward licked his lips as he padded into the next room. The way the bookstore was laid out, he could slip around back and come up behind the fennec, see if he were really reading or if he were daydreaming about some red fox tail.

Daydreaming. Definitely. He sat there staring at the book without turning the page for three whole minutes. Hayward came up behind him and put on his best purr. "That's a pretty good book," he said.

The cutie jumped. "You surprised me," he said.

He had a high voice, but not annoying, and he was definitely gay. Hayward could smell the lust on him. He glanced at the mystery in the fennec's lap, a book he'd never seen before. But he knew the author, knew enough that he knew smart people liked her work. Hayward grinned. "Oh, I'm sorry," he said, stopping his tail from wagging.

They adjourned to the café, where Amir—that was his name—ordered a chai, which Hayward knew Fin liked too. He mocked Hayward's caramel extra-foam latte the way Fin would have, and he told Hayward he'd come up here from the southwest to study urban planning at Pinewood. Better and better. "I know someone who teaches in the architecture school there," he told Amir.

"Really? I'm taking a couple architecture classes next term."

"Keep an eye out for a skinny beaver who dresses in the latest thrift store chic. Dr. Kilgore. He's great, though." Nice cock, and despite the way he dressed, he always kept himself clean.

"I'll remember that. I hear I have to become a hockey fan, too."

"You don't have to. Only if you want to be able to talk to half the people in this town for more than five minutes."

Amir grinned at him. "You're a fan?"

"A casual fan." Hayward sipped his coffee. "I root for the Pioneers 'cause I know one of the players. The Gateway pro team," he clarified to Amir's questioning look.

"Really? How'd you meet him?"

"Through a tenor on the Gay League Chorus." Almost literally, in fact. He let his smile curve wider as he saw Amir relax and smile. "You didn't really doubt, did you?"

"Not really." Amir looked around. Very cute, that he was worried about people overhearing. "I figured it would be too much of a tragedy to waste that body on vixens."

Hayward, surprised, had to laugh. Oh, he liked this one. "And I knew from the way you were looking at me."

He waved off Amir's apology and asked him about his living situation. The fennec was up here on his own, from a town called Viyajo, in which he'd apparently had at least a few anonymous blow jobs which he was embarrassed to discuss. But he mentioned a gay bar, which meant he'd been out in public, so he wasn't a chronic closet case. Hayward flipped through his mental index of stories and told him the one about him and the skunk going at it in the hallway of a hotel. He left out the part with the naked ferret, mainly because the ferret had been smelly and creepy, and somehow that always crept into Hayward's tone and ruined the story.

But Amir didn't flinch at the idea of the public hallway sex, and when Hayward asked him out to dinner, the fennec smiled and agreed right away. "You like Mediterranean?"

"Sure." Amir grinned. "My mom's from there."

"Well, I hope you like Gateway-style Mediterranean. Guaranteed to be 50% blander than the real thing." Hayward smiled at Amir's laugh. "Cafe Ankara isn't too bad. It's near here, over on Mitchell and 45th. Want me to write down the address?"

Amir held up his cell phone, keying in the name. "I think I got it. What time?"

"Seven-thirty okay?"

"Perfect." The fennec smiled. "I'll see you there."

Hayward made arrangements for Fin to meet them there at seven-fifteen, which left him forty-five minutes to go three blocks. It wasn't worth going home and then to the café, so he skimmed his address book on his way to the small lounge across the street. He texted Carmila to let her know he had dinner plans, and Alexi to let him know he'd be at the party, just a little late. Daniel called in the middle of that text to tell him about a wine and cheese he and Xavy were having Saturday afternoon, and Kevin called in the middle of *that* to invite him skating next weekend. And then a stocky wolf down the bar bought him a drink, so there was some flirting before he established that the wolf was married and just looking for a quick blow. And a little flirting after, just because. By the time he finished his text message to Alexi, it was five after seven, so he grabbed his coat, tipped the coat checker, who was a cute little deer mouse, chatted him up enough to get that his name was Colin and he was not single, and walked across to Café Ankara.

He was the first to arrive. "Hi, Shameri," he said to the deer at the hostess stand, slinging his overcoat over his arm. "Table for three."

She beamed back at him. "Right this way."

Hayward followed her to a table near the wall. "How's business? New owners happy?"

"Picking up," she said. "They haven't made any big changes."

"Good," he said. "Don't ever get rid of the house chicken."

She laughed. "Do you want some pita or will you wait?"

"I'll wait," he said, getting out his phone again to tell Alexi that how late depended on how well the rest of the evening went. *Hope I don't see you 'til one,* the ermine responded, which made Hayward smile, and he typed back that it wouldn't be later than midnight, finishing just as Fin walked in.

The swift fox looked as dapper as he could, which meant he'd thrown on a vest over his work clothes. It worked on him, though, because he really had the build for it: tall and lean, but not rail-thin. He brushed Hayward's muzzle with his own before he sat, and smiled across at the fox. Hayward always felt a little tingle at Fin's dusty, spicy musk; the fox smelled like prairie springtime, all full of promise and buds aching to burst open.

The waiter came over to fill the water glass, so Hayward ordered the cabernet and a third wine glass. He saw the set of Fin's ears, and to deflect the fox from complaining about the date, asked him about the play he was in. Fin was taking a supporting role in this one, again pleading work responsibilities, and that distracted him long enough that he only got as far as being disapproving of Hayward's whole date setup before Amir walked in.

Happily, Amir had dressed up some. There was at least a foot difference in height between him and Fin, but when they stood to greet each other, Hayward could definitely see them together. Amir's light fur would set off the dark streaks and patterns, and he could nestle right into Fin's chest. The vision was so clear that he had to remind himself that he'd had clear visions before, when things hadn't worked out. *It promises to be a good night,* he told himself, *and that's enough for now. Things will go further later if they're meant to.*

At least Amir took Fin's unexpected appearance in stride, even if Hayward could tell he didn't quite understand it. And the dinner conversation was pleasant and even fun. Fin had theater stories, of course, and Amir talked about Viyajo. Hayward chimed in when he could, mostly watching the interplay between the two of them and smoothing over when the conversation stalled, or taking an opportunity to embarrass Fin. He kept trying to get Fin's read on Amir, and finally the swift fox gave him an approving nod. It was funny, because he knew Fin had made up his mind about Amir already and was just trying to annoy him by delaying.

When the food arrived, he tried the house chicken to make sure it was spectacular as always, and then offered Amir a bite. The fennec hesitated before accepting. "Oh, if you're sure..." It was cute, but he understood, the whole sharing food thing was kind of intimate. Honey, he said to himself as Amir took the bite, if you didn't want to share food, I wouldn't be getting hard thinking about taking you into that bathroom in about ten minutes.

Amir shared his dish, an orange chicken stew, and Fin offered tastes of his yogurt chicken as well. Hayward had tried them all, but he tasted them to be polite, and to build up that intimacy between the three of them. "I've been going here for months," Hayward told Amir. "There's another Mediterranean place across town, but I think Ankara is better." He looked across at Fin with a slight smile.

"Baghmaria has better kebobs," Fin said, predictably.

"This is all great." Amir sopped up some stew with a piece of warm pita. "My mom's cooking was the best, of course, but she didn't do that much. My dad didn't like it. I only ever went out for Mediterranean a couple times in Chevali. Not much in Viyajo but taquerias and burger joints. Well, there was one Ethiopian place. My friends and I were the only ones who went there who weren't related to the owners, I think."

Adventurous, Hayward thought. Another good sign. "We have a couple of those here. I like 'em, but they're a little spicy for Fin."

"I don't mind spice."

Hayward lowered his eyelids just a bit. "I'm sure you don't," he said. Amir blinked, knitting his brow in a slight frown as though trying to translate what Hayward had said, while Fin rolled his eyes. Hayward just went on eating, and after a moment, the others followed suit.

Once the dinner plates were cleared, Amir sat back in his chair. "Full," he sighed, patting his stomach. "That was a lot of food."

"Sure was." Hayward met Fin's eye, and the swift fox nodded, flagging down the waiter to ask about something on the dessert menu. "I'm going to hit the head."

He got up slowly, waiting for Amir to look at him, and then jerked his head toward the restroom. The fennec's eyes widened.

Hayward didn't let his grin reach his muzzle, not too far. He just raised his eyebrows. Amir's jaw opened, just a little, the expression so cute and eager that Hayward's already-warm sheath gave a little jump. He gave the fennec a quick nod and another jerk of the head, then walked slowly off, letting his tail flow behind him and swinging his hips just enough.

To the delight of the hardness in his sheath, he heard a chair scrape back, and then paws hurrying behind him. Hayward slipped inside the restroom, glanced around to make sure nobody was watching, then called to Amir, who still had that *am I being Punk'd?* look on his muzzle, "Coming?"

Inside, Hayward slammed the door and bolted it, and then pressed Amir up against it, tasting that desert spice in the fennec's fur as he licked along the short muzzle, paws caressing down his sides. He felt the fennec tense, and pulled back. "This okay?"

He could feel that it was, and Amir took a breath before answering, "Yeah. Just surprised me."

"Good." Hayward bent forward to lick back to the fluffy cheek ruff, breathing out softly and waiting for Amir to make the next move.

He didn't have to wait long. The fennec dropped his paws to Hayward's waist and pulled him close. Hayward angled his hips so he could feel the bulge he knew was at Amir's groin, rubbing his own into the fennec in return. More intoxicating than wine, that feeling of getting to know someone new, of an attractive body pressed against his.

And of course, the various things he could play with to see what effect they had. "Every fennec I've ever known," he whispered, breathing into Amir's large, attentive ear, "likes his ears played with." He was basing that all off of his one night with Soki, but from the way Amir's ear was vibrating at his nearness, he was willing to bet it was true. He extended his tongue just enough to brush the fine fur there, and at the answering squeak from Amir, he perked his own ears. "I guess I have a trend," he said.

Amir didn't seem capable of answering, so Hayward forged boldly on, slipping his paw down to feel the shape of Amir's erection through his thin pants. He rubbed the heel of his paw against it. "A definite trend," he murmured, and waited to see if Amir would reach down and return the favor. If he did, Hayward would have to resist the very strong temptation to finish him right here in the bathroom and trust that someone so excited would be ready again once they got to Fin's.

Fortunately, all Amir did was reach down and grab Hayward's rear, which was nice enough and told Hayward that Amir was willing to let him run things. And that was just fine. He drew his fingers up the hard ridge of the fennec's pants, trying to feel the shape, tensing for Amir's paws. While he rubbed Amir, he pressed further into the large, twitching ear, giving it nice, long licks and enjoying the ripples that he could feel in the fennec's body at each lick, at each press of his paw against the straining erection. It was nice, the shape of it, and almost familiar, but not quite, not any more than any of the others were.

But it wasn't the shape, after all, it was the reaction, and from the breathy squeaking that Amir was making, Hayward figured he didn't have a whole lot more playing left before it got serious. So he stopped, pressed in close, and said, "Maybe we should move this somewhere more...private?"

Amir made some vaguely affirmative noises and nodded, still trembling. Hayward smiled and adjusted his pants, looking down at Amir's very visible arousal. Hayward's vest dropped just low enough that it concealed his own, but then, he was more experienced at this. He also cared less if people noticed. "You ready to go back?" he teased.

"Maybe...a minute." The fennec was still gulping for air, but his ears had stopped flicking and he was regaining some composure.

But even three minutes later, the bulge of his sheath was as obvious as ever. Hayward could hear someone outside waiting. "Time for plan B," he said, and moved Amir around behind him, keeping the arch of his tail right at the fennec's waist level.

Amir got the idea quickly. When Hayward opened the door into the face of a lion who went from annoyed to surprised in point six seconds, Amir stayed close behind him. Hayward flashed the lion a grin and a raised eyebrow, and saw not even a flicker of interest before he pushed past them and shut the door of the restroom. Ah, well, some people really were straight, he reminded himself.

Fin did a good job of pretending not to notice anything, though Amir could almost have knocked over a water glass with his hard-on. "Hopefully the date isn't over," the swift fox said.

"It's just getting started," Hayward replied. "So, your place okay?"

Amir still hadn't quite figured out what was going on, but he would. "Sure," Fin said.

The fennec was looking back and forth between them. Hayward rested a paw on his knee, fingers still warm with the memory of the fennec's erection. "Don't be so worried," he said. "If you want to go home, you can."

Amir swallowed. "No, I'm okay," he said.

Hayward smiled. "Did you drive?"

"Took the bus."

He looked across the table at Fin. "Then I guess you have the only car."

Even though Hayward and Amir chose to squeeze into the back of Fin's little compact together, they didn't do anything through their overcoats for the short drive back to Fin's place. Hayward could feel Amir's tension, and he did once or twice lean over to point out things and end up saying something softly into Amir's ear, but that was just to keep the fennec warmed up. The car was pretty chilly, after all. November in Gateway wasn't as bad as December, or January, or February, but it was still colder than just about anywhere else in the country got all winter.

When they got to Fin's place, Hayward felt like warming himself up right away. Fin always kept his apartment a little chilly, having grown up out on the lonesome prairie, so Hayward dragged Amir right to the couch and sat him at one end, plopping down beside him. While Fin was getting them some wine, he flipped on the TiVo. It was nice to have something going on in the background, he'd found, because the appearance of something else going on eased the pressure of the evening being all about the sex.

Which it was, and he'd returned his fingers to Amir's thigh before Fin had even gotten over to them with the wine, but he'd have been content to spend a little longer making out. It was obvious to his nose and eyes, though, that Amir was more than ready for things to get nice and warm, and so he leaned over and breathed some words into the fennec's ear.

Amir went gratifyingly tense, as Hayward felt the weight of Fin settle behind him. He flicked his tail over toward the swift fox and he slid his paw to Amir's stomach. Amir sucked it in as his fingers got close, which was just lovely, and when Hayward did feel the soft fur, he drew his claws through it to the muscles beneath.

It never got old, this part. Even with Fin, if there were no third party, it would be nice, but this was better because he was aware of Fin behind him, and he knew what was coming, and he could still see in his mind's eye the two of them, Amir and Fin, together on this couch without him. He knew Fin would like Amir's body, a physique as lean as his that was well-taken care of, and from the way Amir was groping his thighs and

squeezing the muscles there, he was pretty sure Amir would like Fin's runner's build.

Fin had started stroking Hayward's tail, so Hayward shifted around, nudging Amir into the arm of the futon couch and playing with that delightfully sensitive ear as Amir rubbed up to his chest. His ears flicked back and forth between Amir's panting squeaks and Fin's soft growls as he got himself ready for his part in this.

Amir and Fin were on the same schedule, the fennec pulling Hayward toward him while Fin's paw rubbed insistently at his tail. Hayward's own body was singing like an electric wire, now on the couch on all fours facing Amir. He hiked his tail up, inviting Fin to get going there, feeling the need like an ache inside him. The memory of pine tickled his nose.

Fin chuckled, making Amir notice him, and the fennec's eyes flickered with uncertainty. "Should, uh," he said.

Hayward pulled his head back from the fennec's ear and grinned. He brought one paw back to Amir's lap, cupping his erection and starting to free it. "Don't worry," he said. "Fin's got plenty to occupy him."

Fin did indeed. Hayward felt the swift fox's fingers at his pants, opening them at the same time as he opened Amir's, diving inside, fingers closing around his thick shaft as he wrapped his fingers around Amir's. The fennec gasped, squeaked, and made that directionless rubbing with his paw around Hayward's stomach that guys make when they're being attended to and they feel like they have to do something in return. Hayward watched Amir's shaft emerge in his black fingers. Nice, long, and clean, with a couple drops of pre beaded at the tip. He slid his fingers up and down, exploring it, looking at the shape. A little thicker than Foster's, but about the same length.

Around then, he realized that Amir's rubbing was not, in fact, directionless, but was moving down his body in an attempt to reach his erection, the one Fin was already rubbing up and down. Hayward was better than Amir at keeping his trembling under control, but his legs were starting to shiver. He kept stroking Amir, though, watching the fennec's face.

Amir's light fingers found Hayward's tip, probably a bit sooner than they were expecting. The fennec's smile turned to wide-eyed surprise when his fingers met Fin's. "I told you," Hayward murmured, wriggling his hips at the feel of two paws on his tense, taut shaft.

"Here," Fin rumbled behind him, and Hayward felt his paw reach out, take the smaller fennec's fingers, and press them around Hayward's length. "Can you hold this for a minute?"

Amir's smile was growing. "Big," he murmured, and that made Hayward smile wider. The little fennec had a nice touch, smooth and gentle, and curious too, those digits sliding along his hot skin tenderly, exploring its shape and heft.

To make Amir think about that cock sliding into him, Hayward said, "That's why I don't top," putting emphasis on the 'top,' or at least, he started to say that, but just as he opened his muzzle, Fin plunged two slippery fingers into him, and he had to suck in his breath. It wasn't just the fingers themselves. It was the prelude, the way their awkward form alerted his body that something much nicer was coming. He shivered, his muzzle still hanging open, and then said his piece.

He was watching Amir think about that, but it was Fin who responded, fingers probing and rubbing. "Oh, is that why?"

Hayward kept Amir's length in his fingers, but had to close his eyes as Fin pulled his fingers out. Anticipation was delicious, though not, in this case, superior to experience. He almost dropped his muzzle then and there, but Amir was looking pretty excited, and he wanted to keep this interesting for everyone for as long as he could. He closed his eyes and for a moment, he was elsewhere, but he only indulged himself for that one moment. Then he forced himself back to the present and smiled at Amir, giving the fennec's cock a nice squeeze. "There may be...other reasons," he said, feeling the warmth of Fin's shaft bobbing near his thighs, the motion of the swift fox getting into position behind him.

"Other reasons, he says." Fin sounded amused, and slightly strained, eager. Hayward was glad he was talking to Amir and including him. The part of his brain that was still thinking about such things thought it boded well. "Just one big reason, I says. And here it comes."

Hayward felt the pressure under his tail then, and let his paw relax around Amir's shaft, not letting go, just settling there while he focused on the slick warmth pushing into him, stretching him and filling him, sliding inside. He heard himself moan inside his head but didn't know if he'd made an actual noise or not. The feel of someone inside him always made him weak, made him shiver, and when it was the heat of someone like Fin, it just made his tail tingle all the way up his spine.

He pushed Amir forward until the fennec's paw slipped off his shaft, leaving it hanging in the chill air. With a smile, he dipped his head and closed his lips around Amir's tip. The salty taste told him that Amir was as excited as he looked, and as he pushed his muzzle further down, Fin reached beneath him and closed a slick paw around Hayward, and the red fox almost jumped despite himself.

Now they were all three moving together, Hayward holding the swift fox's hardness inside him while pushing his muzzle down over Amir's. His lips brushed the knot, which was not quite full yet, so he was able to open his jaw over it and suck hard while rubbing Amir's tip against the roof of his mouth.

Fin was thrusting harder, his own knot too big now to push in without tying. Hayward focused on sliding his muzzle up and down Amir's shaft, letting Fin's stroking and thrusting work their magic on him. Soft whiteness enveloped him as the familiar rhythms slid in and out, Fin's cock almost the right shape, close enough that he knew he wasn't going to last long.

He braced himself and reached up to stroke Amir's ear while his muzzle continued to work, The fennec responded with a series of squeaks, his shaft quivering against Hayward's tongue. The red fox worked both cocks, licking and pressing forward with his muzzle, squeezing and pressing back with his hips, and both foxes pressed back, Fin's rasping pants the counterpoint to Amir's high-pitched squeaks. And even as he took them both in, even as the whiteness folded itself around him, there was a part of him that was thinking about how well they would go together without him in the middle.

But he loved that middle, loved the two warm bodies on either side of him, the hardness in his mouth and under his tail, Fin's paw squeezing tighter as it stroked. And while his body tensed and quivered in the familiar prelude, the scent of pine grew stronger, not from the air, but from memory. And that was how he knew he was close, because it was at those moments of climax that the pine and the whiteness were strongest.

Amir bucked into his muzzle, warmth and passion flooding it as he yelped in climax. Hayward absorbed the smell, the taste, the excitement in the slender desert body arching against him. A moment later, Fin slammed hard into him, warmth spreading from the other end into his hips. The waves of excitement crested in his groin. The smell of pine overwhelmed him.

Oh, he moaned in his head. *Foster…*

And then the world was white.

He opened his eyes to ivory fur and warm musk on his tongue, squeaks of passion still echoing in his ears. He swallowed and licked for more, making Amir squirm, the hardnesses in his muzzle and tail quivering in tandem. Inhaling Amir's dusty scent in, he sagged slightly, the whiteness and pine receding with the glow of orgasm.

But he still felt them as he gulped and pulled his muzzle up, drawing his tongue along Amir's trembling cock. The fennec's muzzle was hanging open, tongue draped over his little teeth. "You're sweet," Hayward told him.

Amir giggled and flicked his large ears. Hayward started to say that he loved Amir's ears, but just then Fin rested a paw on his tail and slid himself out. The release sent another tremor through Hayward's cock, and another spurt of sticky seed onto the sofa. "Oh," he sighed, "they feel almost as good going out as going in." Mischievously, he added, "you think?"

That took Amir by surprise. Hayward saw him start to come down, to feel that post-coital awkwardness. When you weren't actually having sex, being naked with people you'd just met was not nearly as fun. The fennec mumbled something, and so Hayward ruffled his ear. "Aw, sweetie, we're all hanging out together," he said. "No need to be embarrassed."

Fin went to clean up, and that gave Hayward the chance to talk to Amir. He curled his tail under him and scooted next to the fennec on the couch. "Sorry," he said, and inclined a head toward his mess, "but it's a little wet over there." Fin would probably be upset he'd forgotten the cover, but Hayward couldn't help that.

Amir nodded. "It's okay."

He still seemed embarrassed, uncertain. Hayward leaned in, taking care not to let his shaft drip onto the fennec's leg. "I know this is a bit weird," he said, keeping an ear perked to the bathroom, "but trust me, Fin's a really good guy."

"I like him." But his body language didn't back up the words. He edged away from Hayward, and that made Hayward worry for a moment. He'd had it happen before, where the threesome just unsettled a person to the point that he had gotten up and left, and so he was getting ready to say something else when Amir came to a decision on his own. He settled his lithe frame against the red fox, and Hayward was glad to feel him relax.

"I knew you would." Hayward tried not to sound too smug. "You guys hit it off at dinner."

"I guess." He could read Amir's next question before it came out. "You were asking *me* out, right?"

Hayward had to grin at the fox's earnestness. "Of course I was," he said, just as the bathroom door opened. "But I have a lot of friends, and as Fin pointed out, two is better than one."

"But three is not better than two," Fin said, rejoining them.

Hayward edged closer to Amir as the swift fox wiped up the mess he'd left on the couch, and then got up, to leave the two of them alone together. He held out his paw for the towel Fin was holding. "I'm gonna clean up myself. Want me to take that in to the bathroom?"

Fin dropped the towel in his paw and plopped down on the other end of the couch. Hayward hesitated a moment, but that was Fin: not inclined to get too close too fast. Pushing him wouldn't help anything. So he listened to them start talking as he went into the bathroom to wipe off.

There were three texts on his phone, one from Alexi asking when he was going to be there, another from Alexi telling him that Shim, a mutual friend, was leaving for the party in fifteen minutes and could give him a ride if he wanted, and the third from Carmila responding to his text about dinner plans with a simple, "ok." He texted Alexi back that he would meet Shim in fifteen minutes on the corner outside Fin's place.

After wiping off his shaft, sheath, and rear, he sprinkled some scented powder in his fur and rinsed out his muzzle. The echoes of the evening reverberated faintly in his memory, so he closed his eyes and took a moment to hold on to them before going back out into the living room.

Even though he knew Fin wouldn't go, he invited him to the party, and when he declined, Hayward told Amir he was welcome to stay. He saw Fin's amused exasperation, but the swift fox would've been too reticent to invite Amir on his own, and Amir accepted quickly enough that it put a wag in Hayward's tail as he skipped down the stairs.

It had been a good date, and it would've been okay just to go home and enjoy the memory of the night, but Alexi's party would include a number of people Hayward wanted to keep in touch with, and Alexi'd said Boris had invited a co-worker of his that he wanted Hayward to meet. After Fin and Amir, he didn't think he'd be wanting any more physical action tonight, so the small press of people in Alexi's condo would be fine. And Alexi did have a balcony and a laundry room, in case an interesting opportunity did present itself. So he bounced on his paws, licking his lips and wagging his tail over the memory of Amir's and Fin's shafts and how well they'd gotten along—Amir and Fin, not their cocks—until Shim pulled up outside.

Hayward hurried into the car and slid inside. Shim, an older raccoon, sniffed the air as he did. "From one party to another," he said.

"A fox's work is never done." Hayward leaned back and watched the streetlights go by. It was a little difficult going from Fin's and Amir's quiet natures to Shim's complaining, but he only had to listen to the raccoon for ten minutes. He thought about Amir and Fin, talking, slowly growing closer together in the apartment, and thought about Alexi and Boris, and he met Shim's complaints about the fox who lived below him with a smile.

Alexi's condo was on the fourth floor of an old stone building on the corner of Killick and Jefferson. They had to park about two blocks away, which of course rankled Shim. "Fucking yuppies," he growled, smacking the side of a BMW as they walked past it, breath steaming in the air. "Turning this whole neighborhood into some kind of bland, cookie-cutter, upscale shopping mall devoid of soul."

"But they have such lovely clothes," Hayward said. Pity Shim was straight. The old raccoon would be perfect for someone like Alexi. Though of course, Alexi was now taken. But still, Hayward thought they felt the echo of that alternate-universe relationship in their close friendship. Fin also liked Shim, though he said that in any setting other than a party, the raccoon's dourness wore on him after a while.

"Window dressing," Shim growled. "Fancy curtains on an empty room."

"Is that from one of your poems?"

Shim shot him a look. "Don't make fun."

"I'm not." Hayward smiled. "I thought it was really good."

The raccoon relaxed. "It was all right. Think it's from something I read."

"You should write it down." Hayward held the door. "And try to have fun. Alexi will be so sad if you don't."

"His fault for predicating his happiness on factors beyond his control." But Shim was smiling now, at least as much as he ever did, the severe straight line of his mouth quirked up at the corners.

"That's Alexi." Hayward smiled, tail wagging all the way up in the elevator.

Alexi himself met them at the door with effusive hugs and peppermint schnapps breath, draping himself over them like a mustelid body wrap.

"My two favorite people!" he gushed, flowing from one to the other and then back. "Come, it is party!" They could hear music now, and off-key singing.

"Whoo," Shim grimaced, waving at the air. "The party is wherever you are, Lexy."

"Then come join me!" The ermine twirled around and stumbled back into the condo, keeping one paw on the door to swing it shut after Shim and Hayward had come in. "Coats in the bedroom, drinks on the bar." Hayward had trouble following the little black paw as it bobbed and waved, but he knew where the bedroom here was. He took Shim's coat and dropped both in the room, took a moment to fluff up his chest fur (and a discreet sniff to tell that Alexi and Boris were still a happy couple), and walked back out into the living room.

Shim was at the bar getting a drink. Alexi had taken the microphone of the karaoke machine, and was singing, "I Know What Wolves Like," substituting "hares" for "wolves." Hayward started to make his way across the living room to join him, but it was slow going; he knew just about everyone there and had to say hi, and the people he didn't know, he was curious about. He had just introduced himself to a tall coyote with wire-rimmed glasses when someone jerked on his vest. He turned to see a jaguar with slightly unfocused eyes and a green drink.

"Vico," he said with a smile. "I didn't know you'd be here."

"I been missing you," the jaguar said. He lowered his voice to what he no doubt thought was a discreet whisper. "Missin' that sweet mouth."

Hayward turned to the coyote, whose eyes had narrowed slightly. "Excuse me a second," he said. "I'm so sorry about this."

The coyote smiled and nodded, moving away. Hayward turned to face Vico, who pushed insistently at him. "C'mon," he said. "Bedroom is free. We got ten minutes."

"I was just heading over to get a drink," Hayward said. "Why don't you let me get one and then we'll take care of you?"

"Oh, sure," Vico said. "I could use 'nother drink m'self."

"You've got one right there." Hayward said, amused.

"What, this?" Vico downed the rest of it in one gulp and set the empty glass down on a coffee table.

Hayward smiled for Vico's benefit, following the jaguar to the bar, where Boris greeted him with a wave. The snowshoe hare had his thick winter coat in, black patches on his shoulders and ears the only marks in the thick white fur. "Hay!" he said, and stepped around the bar for a hug. "It has been too long. Where have you been hiding yourself?"

"Work," Hayward said. "And everything else. But I wouldn't miss one of your parties. How's the bookkeeping business?"

"The books, they will not keep themselves." The hare laughed, and reached for a wine bottle. "Your usual?"

"Please. And another of whatever Vico was having."

"And h-hurry up," Vico said. "We got business of our own."

Boris's whiskers twitched, his eyes meeting Hayward's. Hayward inclined his head subtly, so Boris went ahead and poured another green concoction for Vico, and then a glass of white wine for Hayward. "There is someone here I had hoped you could meet," he said slowly to Hayward. "I think he may be leaving soon."

Hayward smiled and took the glass. He turned to Vico and nuzzled the jaguar. "Honey," he said in a low voice, "just let me go see this guy, and I'll be right back."

"You said we were gonna go," Vico whined, a little too loudly. "C'mon, Hay, what's up?" He lowered a paw to cup his own groin. "Just ten minutes, c'mon." A couple people turned to look, but this was one of Alexi's parties, after all, and they knew Hayward.

"You've waited three weeks, you can wait another fifteen minutes." He touched the jaguar's nose with a finger. "I'll be back. You just enjoy that drink."

"Don't tease me," Vico said.

"It will be a minute," Boris leaned in as he said it, and Vico stepped back and out of the way, his ears flat.

"What should I do about Vico?" Boris asked as they walked over there, his voice soft so that only Hayward's ears could pick it up over the music.

"Let him finish his drink," Hayward said. "He'll pass out soon. Just keep an eye on him. Don't let him leave."

Boris nodded, and stopped behind a tall canid, brown ears perked, wearing jeans and a long-sleeved white cotton shirt. Hayward recognized the older coyote with the glasses a moment before he turned around in response to Boris's tap. "Kinzi," Boris said, "This is Hayward, the fox I was telling you about."

Kinzi arched an eyebrow and smiled. Behind his glasses, dark brown eyes glinted. "Has it been ten minutes already?"

Hayward laughed. Nice sense of humor. "Boris insisted I come back here."

"Hayward is in travel industry," the hare said. "He is genius at matching right person with right package."

"Is that so?" Kinzi smiled.

"The trick," Hayward said, "is to pick one that's just the right length. A vacation, I mean. You want to come home wishing you'd had one more day, so the memories are always fond."

"I see." Kinzi's tail swished. "How do you know what's the right length for the right person?"

Boris rested a paw on the red fox's shoulder. "That is Hay's genius."

Kinzi chuckled at Hayward's flicked ears. "As it happens, I have some vacation time coming up and I was just wondering what to do with it."

Boris lifted his paw and raised it in farewell, leaving to attend to the bar. Hayward patted the hare's shoulder and looked up at the coyote. "Just you, or…"

"Just me," Kinzi said. "I'm recently, ah, un-partnered."

"So sorry to hear that," Hayward said. He felt a familiar twinge. "Looking to explore some new horizons?"

"Absolutely." The lenses of the coyote's glasses flickered with reflections as he ducked his head. "I never traveled much with Jake. If you're in a relationship, you know about the sacrifices you have to make."

It was a question as much as a statement. Hayward inclined his head. "There are drawbacks to being single, too," he said. No sense giving it all away this soon.

"I'm familiar with those." The coyote's muzzle twisted. "I'm trying to focus on the benefits."

Hayward took a drink, and smiled. The coyote's dry matter-of-fact manner reminded him of a lion he'd known a few years ago. He consulted his mental rolodex and found a list of names he'd come up with for the lion, many of whom would have worked as well as the mate he'd ended up with. A familiar voice read off a couple who'd go well with the coyote. He reached into his vest pocket and took out a business card. "I'm sure I can help. Why don't you call me on Monday and we can talk business?"

Kinzi looked at the card. "Oh, you're close to my office."

"Well, we could meet over lunch, too." Hayward started to lift the glass to his lips again, but as he did, a paw grabbed his arm, spilling half the wine over the floor.

"Hey!" Vico's voice was loud enough to pin his ears back. "You said you'd be back."

The murmur of conversation around them died down. "Honey," Hayward started, trying to pull his arm free, but Vico held it tight.

"Don't 'honey' me. You said you'd take care of me and now you're chatting up this fucker?" Vico's breath reeked of melon. Hayward wouldn't have thought he could get that drunk on Midori.

"I haven't forgotten about you," he said, resting his paw over Vico's.

"F-fuckin' cocktease!" The jaguar yelled it, and that brought the conversation in the room to a halt.

"Now," Kinzi said in his deep, calm voice. "Let's be polite."

"You stay outta this." Vico barely glanced at him, shrugging him off. His green eyes bored into Hayward's. "C-come on. Let's go."

After all that Hayward had tried to do for him, had he not changed at all? He didn't appreciate anything. Hayward heard Foster's calm voice telling him, *he's just a kid, he doesn't know any better.* The red fox willed his hackles to go down, seeing the world through the jaguar's eyes. He could get him off, and it would not disrupt Alexi's party, and then he would send Vico home in a cab.

"All right," he said quietly. He ran his tongue around the inside of his mouth. "Go see if the bedroom is free."

Vico's muzzle broke out in a grin, and he clapped Hayward on the shoulder. The grin turned to a worried frown as something over Hayward's shoulder caught his eyes. "Come on, let's go now."

"Just a minute." Kinzi placed a paw on Hayward's shoulder. "We were having a nice conversation. I'd rather like to finish it."

"It's okay," Hayward said, but Vico's eyes, fixed on Kinzi now, narrowed.

"Fuck off," the jaguar snarled. This time, Kinzi didn't back down. He turned to Vico and stepped closer, looking down from his height advantage. The jaguar's ears flattened. Again, he looked over Hayward's shoulder, and then stuttered, "H-he's coming with me. He said."

"Doesn't look like he wants to." Kinzi had managed, smoothly, to stand between Hayward and Vico. The jaguar took one more look over Hayward's shoulder and then turned and tried to bolt.

He'd waited too long. Hayward felt the motion Boris made before he heard or saw him; the hare swept silently past him and spun Vico forcibly around. The jaguar's protest died on his lips, his mouth hanging open as he looked at the hare's laid-back ears and slit-thin eyes. He didn't resist as Boris pushed him toward the kitchen, behind the bar.

The crowd watched them go. Hayward smiled slightly; despite his aspirations to be sympathetic, he almost wished he could watch the hare light into the jaguar, just for the spectacle. It was easier to feel sorry for Vico from a distance, but there were lines and rules of behavior that one just did not cross. "Sorry about that," he said to Kinzi, and to the others who were watching. And to Foster, too. And then, only to Kinzi, he said, "and thanks."

The coyote smiled. "Glad I could help."

Alexi had made his way to his side, and if the ermine had been a little tipsy before, he was dead sober now. "Well," he said, "he can kiss his Christmas party invitation bye-bye."

"No, no," Hayward said. "Just keep track of how much he drinks. I'm surprised he hasn't passed out already."

"I won't have this kind of scene at my parties. It's so negative."

Hayward grinned around. "Oh, look at everyone talking. It'll be *the* topic of conversation for months."

"I'm pleased to have been here to witness it," Kinzi said dryly.

Alexi's gaze flicked up to the tall coyote. "We will see," he said. "If he listens to Boris...maybe."

He wandered back toward the kitchen, but Hayward saw him stop and talk to one of the other guests, and then another joined them. Alexi gesticulated with his black paws, re-telling the story animatedly. Sympathetic smiles came his way. If it came to sides, and reputations, the people here knew him well enough.

Behind Hayward, Kinzi's gruff voice said, "So, what is your deal?"

Hayward turned to see Kinzi's half-smile. "Usually it takes a couple dates for someone to ask me that," he said.

"I would say this little scene counts as at least a date and a half."

"For you," Hayward said. He inclined his head and perked his ears in a listening pose.

Kinzi's smile grew. "Fair enough." He glanced around, and lowered his voice with his ears. "I left Jake after thirteen years because we'd grown apart; we were only staying together out of habit. I've been on two dates since then and only went to bed with one of them."

"Also, he was cheating on you."

Behind his glasses, the coyote's eyes widened briefly. "You know Jake?" Suspicion clouded his features. "Did you...?"

Hayward shook his head. "You remind me of a guy I knew a while ago. He broke up with his boyfriend, too, and he said it was because things got boring. But he liked stability, and consistency, so I made a few…discreet inquiries." He coughed. "His boyfriend was seeing other people. That's why things got boring. I'd wager your Jake was looking to spice things up elsewhere too. You sound like someone who likes stability, but also values loyalty."

Kinzi stared at him and then shook his head. "I've never gone on two dates in less than fifteen minutes before," he said.

Hayward winked. "I move fast."

"Fast enough for dinner instead of lunch?"

Hayward inclined his head. "I think I'm free Tuesday night." He'd have the weekend to try to track down the person he thought would work, and if he weren't free, there was nothing wrong with a get-to-know-him better dinner. Or a get-to-know-him hand job. Come to think of it, that'd be a nice way to wash off the memory of Vico's shouting. "Or we could go grab something now?"

"I'm a bit tired," Kinzi said, with a smile. "And you just got here."

"Oh, they're used to me not staying long." Hayward tapped his phone, which was blinking. "Always things to do."

Kinzi's eyebrow arched. "Things?"

Hayward laughed. "I like you," he said. *I'll find you someone nice, someone who won't cheat on you.*

"So, look," the coyote said. "Before I go…could this go anywhere?" He motioned back and forth between himself and Hayward. "I don't care about people's pasts."

Hayward smiled. "There's a definite chance."

As Kinzi took his leave, Alexi came up beside Hayward. "A definite chance?" he repeated. "Oh ho, so perhaps you may finally be settling down?"

Hayward brushed Alexi's short tail with his own. "I'll definitely settle *him* down," he said. "How's Vico?"

Alexi shook his head. "Afraid of Boris. Come on, Kinzi's nice, isn't he? Jake's a whore. Kinzi deserves someone better."

Hayward almost laughed at the ermine's earnest melodrama. Instead, he kissed him on the cheek. "I know. I saw Benki and Alan here earlier. How are they doing?"

"Hay," Alexi said, "you know nobody believes that. What Vico was saying. You know, right? We don't think you're a slut."

"It's okay," Hayward said. "I am a slut."

Alexi's eyes filled with moisture. Perhaps he wasn't as sober as he seemed. "Vi *angyel,*" he whispered, throwing his arms around Hayward and pressing his little muzzle to the crook of the red fox's neck.

"Hush," Hayward said, patting him on the back. "I'm just well connected."

"So well connected, you should find yourself someone," the ermine murmured as he released Hayward.

"I've got someone. Tell me about Benki and Alan. Did they work out the thing with Alan's mom?"

Alexi's stubborn look didn't fade, but he told Hayward about Benki and Alan, and then two other couples they knew. When the party began to wind down, Hayward sat with Alexi and Boris and listened to how they were doing, and then accepted Alexi's offer to drive him home.

They chattered most of the way back about coffee shops and restaurants and the new store at the mall, and Hayward promised to come to dinner at their place sometime. "And bring someone special," Alexi said as the fox got out, wrapping his overcoat around him. "Just one."

Hayward grinned. "Thanks for the ride, hon, and the party."

"I am sorry again about Vico." Alexi rolled his eyes, getting out on his side. He walked around to Hayward. "Find that boy someone, yes?"

"Working on it." They hugged, and then Hayward waved and walked into the hallway of his building. The light from the street vanished abruptly as the door swung shut, but he knew his way well enough even if he hadn't been able to see the ghostly outline of the doorframes and the lighter numbers on the doors. He touched a paw to his door as he slid the key in, stifling a yawn.

Though it was after one in the morning, the light on the desk of the small living room was on. The short arctic fox in the wheelchair didn't look up from the open textbook as Hayward walked in and locked the door behind him. Her presence there was as fixed a part of the room as the paintings that had come with the apartment, the glass coffee table, the couch and chair. The TV sat alone against the far wall, no shelves of DVDs and CDs like at Fin's; neither of them collected movies, and all of Carm's music was on her computer.

"Up late studying?" he said, hanging his coat up in the closet. He dropped his vest over the arm of the stuffed chair and lifted his nose. No outside scents intruded, with the window closed against the chill November night.

"Up late fucking?" Her voice was raspy, her tone bored. "Clothes in the hamper."

Hayward grinned and picked up the vest, walking it to the bathroom, where he dropped it in the hamper. "You're the second person to ask me that tonight. Actually, I was at a remarkably restrained party at Alexi's." She didn't answer. "He and Boris are still together. Doing very well."

She turned a page in the book. "Course they are," she said.

He walked over to the desk, looking down at the thick masses of legal text on the page. Beside the book, a laptop computer was open to a search result page, illuminating her white fur with a blue tinge. As usual, she wore a collared shirt hanging open at the front, and a blanket across her lap. She and the clothes smelled clean, but he caught a whiff of old must, maybe from the dust on her wheels. She had washed herself, but not the chair. "I thought you had Friday afternoon off."

"I took a nap. Didn't get any studying done."

He fingered a green sticker on her wheelchair, with the current date on it. "Mm-hmm. And the security guards at the courthouse came up during your nap to check your chair for weapons."

When she didn't answer, he said, "Carm?"

"Research," she muttered. Hayward sighed. Before he could say anything, she said, "Don't start. Every case is different."

"Drunk driving cases have nuance?"

Now she flicked her ears back. "Those boys you fuck, do they have 'nuance'?"

Hayward rested a paw on the base of his tail. "Some of them do."

"I had the time to spare," she said.

"What about 'look forward, not back'?"

"I told you not to start. I need to get three more precedents read tonight so I only have twenty to read this weekend." She tapped one claw on the book. "And if we're talking about 'look forward,' when are you going to stop setting up other people and start looking for yourself?"

She didn't really understand that he didn't need someone else. But it wasn't worth having the argument again. He was tired. "Did you eat?"

"Your leftover pasta from last night."

"Why don't you get some rest?" He gestured to the book. "The cases will still be there in the morning."

"If I don't know these precedents for the test on Monday," she said, and she didn't need to finish. He nuzzled her ears. She flicked them back.

Hayward sighed again. "One more semester," he said, as much to himself as to her, and walked back to the kitchen. "Anything I can get you?"

"Coffee," she called. "There's cookies there if you want one."

He smelled the aroma of baking before he saw the plate. Chocolate chip coconut—his favorite. He chewed one and knelt by the low cupboard to take out Carmila's favorite dark roast. As he shook it into the filter, he said, "What did he get?"

"She," she said. He set the filter in the machine and bent to fill the reservoir from the filtered water pitcher in the sink. The counters were low, so that Carmila could get the coffee herself when it was ready. She could make it, too, but it was a pain to maneuver in the small kitchen. As he turned the machine on, she said, "It was a beaver, Hay."

The coffee machine gurgled. The sweetness of the cookie soured. For a moment, he saw very clearly the image in his head, the middle-aged beaver with grey creeping around the bridge of her muzzle, one ear notched from some domestic fight, her shrill voice edged with resentment even as she broke down in a sobbing apology. "She wasn't even crying," Carmila said from the other room.

Hayward watched the drip of the coffee. Again, he heard Foster's calm voice telling him he couldn't hold on to the anger, telling him to remember the joy and spread it. His eyes slid upward, to a shelf Carmila couldn't see onto, to a photo of an arctic fox with a wide smile. The joy in his bright blue eyes, like a negative image of Carm's dark, flat blue eyes, made Hayward wish again that Carm could take more than just pain from the photos. "I'm sure she felt terrible," he said.

"She got her license suspended," Carmila said. "By the book."

"I went out with a new guy tonight," Hayward said. He took out a mug and set it by the coffee maker, and grabbed one more cookie. "Coffee'll be ready in a minute."

Carmila had turned from her computer, looking at him as he walked out of the kitchen. "A ferret was put in the hospital."

He ate the rest of the cookie without tasting it. Walking over to her, he crouched down, even though he knew that annoyed her. "You'd like this new guy. He's a fennec. He's sweet."

"Don't patronize me," she snapped. "Don't you care?"

"I don't know the ferret," he said. "I feel sorry for him, but I don't know him. You can't get this worked up about random cases like this."

She spun away from him, back to the computer. "It's not random."

"Just focus on law school," he said. "That's constructive."

"Easy for you," she said. "You go out wherever you want."

"You want to go somewhere?"

"No." She pulled herself over to the book and bent over it, shutting him out.

He sighed, standing. If only there were someone he could find for her. He rested his paws on her shoulders, and she didn't tense, but she didn't stop studying, either. "Let's have dinner tomorrow night," he said. "I'll make reservations somewhere."

"Sure." She said it absently, as if she were just reading, but he knew she was trying to distance herself from him and the situation. She'd be in a better mood tomorrow night for dinner. For now, the best thing to do was leave her alone.

He'd gotten almost to his bedroom when she asked, "How was the new guy? The fennec?"

Hayward ran his tongue around the inside of his mouth. "Delicious."

Carmila snorted. "Do you like him?"

"I set him up with Fin."

"Is that the grumpy raccoon guy?"

"That's Shim," Hayward said. "Fin's a swift fox. Theater guy."

"Don't know how you keep them all straight. I mean," she said quickly, "how you remember them all."

Hayward smiled. "I don't know how you remember all those cases. But I think Amir will work with Fin. Maybe. I'm optimistic."

"Good," she said, and turned another page in her book. "I'm sick of hearing about him."

"I met someone else tonight."

"Oh, God."

"He's an older coyote. His partner was cheating on him and he's single now."

"Don't tell me his name."

"It's Kinzi. He's sweet."

"Are you going to date him?"

He rubbed his ears. "I'm going to find someone nice for him."

"Good night, Hay."

Hayward smiled. "G'night, sis."

She raised a paw as he left the room. He stripped off his pants and boxers in the bathroom, tossed them in the hamper, and clambered up over the wide double bed that had once been his to the narrow loft. On the shelf next to his head as he stretched out, another small photo rested in a pine-scented frame. He looked at his own expression, four years younger, dreamy and carefree, and then at Foster's, alert and protective. He touched the nose of the arctic fox. "I'm trying to help her, sweetheart," he whispered. "Goodnight." He rolled back onto his back, but even after he'd closed his eyes, the picture stayed clear and luminous in his head.

CHAPTER 3.5:
HOW TO GET THROUGH THE DAY

How to get through the day:
1. *Pills.*
2. *Set goals.*
3. *Keep your mind busy with something you enjoy.*
4. *When people ask how you are, say "Good" rather than "Okay." Even if you don't feel it.*
5. *Do not talk about how you really feel.*
6. *Resist the urge to isolate yourself.*
7. *Do something good for someone else.*
8. *Exercise.*
9. *Commend yourself for something you did well today.*
10. *Tomorrow will be a good day.*

9. Commend yourself for something you did well today.

Fin hung up his vest and touched the sticker on the inside of his closet, reading the words as he did every night. *Something you did well today.* The swift fox unbuttoned his shirt. It hadn't been a bad day, but it hadn't been a particularly good one. Work was work, a dreary monotony of forms and reports and meetings. There'd been no theater rehearsal. He'd resisted the tempting chocolate chip cookies at lunch. There was that.

He tossed his shirt into the hamper and slid a paw down his side. He could afford a few more cookies, to be honest. The memory of his 220-pound self might be persistent, but it was only a memory. Still, indulgence led to habit, as his counselor used to tell him.

There was the call with Amir, setting up another Hay date for tomorrow. That was an indulgence, but it hadn't yet become a habit. He let his mind linger on the memory of the last one, leaning back in the corner of his couch getting sucked off while watching Amir's muzzle contort as he fucked the slender red fox. Hayward was good with his tongue, and it was fun watching the little fennec top him, too. Fin had made sure to lay down towels on the couch this time, so he didn't have to throw the cushion cover in the laundry after.

When Amir'd gone to clean up, Hayward had asked how much Fin had seen of the fennec, and had chided him gently when Fin said 'a couple times for coffee.' Really, though Fin appreciated the Hay dates, of course, what business was it of his? But the post-orgasmic warmth kept Fin from voicing those thoughts; he merely said things were moving at their own pace, and that he didn't see Hayward complaining about having a regular setup.

Fin slid his pants off and threw them into the hamper as well. He brushed a finger along the outline of his sheath, through his boxers. Neither the memory of last week's Hay date nor the anticipation of tomorrow was stirring it much.

He walked over to his bed. *Something you did well today.* He wasn't allowed to lie down until he'd come up with something. No cheating.

He'd made a good breakfast. He remembered that now. He'd bought fresh onions yesterday on the way home, had grated fresh cheese, and the omelette had been pretty good. Better than good; he hadn't burned it or made much of a mess. He'd thought that if he didn't do anything else well today, he could count that. In retrospect, it seemed like the most tangible success. *Good breakfast*, he told himself, and lay down.

10. Tomorrow will be a good day.

Maybe he would try cooking dinner tomorrow, he thought. Hay always wanted to go out to dinner, but Fin could probably talk him and Amir into a home-cooked meal. He could pick up some more fresh vegetables on the way home, maybe a roasted chicken, and he could make a casserole. He hadn't made one of those in a while, just because it was hard to make one small enough for one, and he never finished leftovers.

That sounded good. They'd been out enough times that it would be nice to have a quiet evening at home instead of going out. And he could pick up a pie on the way home. Apple maybe. He didn't know what Hay liked. Although he remembered Amir liked cherries. Cherry pie, then. Hay probably wouldn't stay for dessert anyway. Fin imagined Hay saying, *it depends on what you call 'dessert,' honey.* He chuckled and closed his eyes.

1. Pills.

Two small blue pills, a glass of juice. A bowl of cold cereal. Fin was out of eggs, but that was okay. He didn't have to make an omelet every morning. He sat down at the dining room table, feeling darkly unsettled as he always did until the pills kicked in. It wasn't a physical sensation, rather a sort of desperation, as though every action he took was a struggle against an enormous pressure to lie down on the floor. He always took the pills first, finding a symbolic comfort in them even before the weight lifted, which usually happened before he finished eating.

The action of dropping the pills on his tongue and picking up his orange juice had taken on the familiarity of a ritual. He swallowed, facing the window. The reflection of his collared shirt and brown vest showed ghostlike over the creeping progress of the sun above the roofs of the buildings across the street. The chill tang of the orange juice faded slowly from his tongue. He picked up his spoon and dipped it into the cereal.

When he was done eating, he sat back in his chair. His tail twitched, then began to swish back and forth.

2. Set goals.

Today he was going to go to the market and get the ingredients for the casserole, but first he was going to have to call Hay and talk the fox into eating a home-cooked meal for once. He had two reports to look over at work, too, but those were routine. Cooking a casserole would be challenging. Talking Hayward into a change in his routine would be, probably, impossible. But then again, you never knew, with Hay. He flitted from one engagement to another with mercurial abandon. If Fin could be persuasive, and not just obdurate, then Hay would be more likely to listen. Fin could do it. He *would* do it.

3. Keep your mind busy with something you enjoy.

Fin's job as a compliance consultant (more precisely, as a junior member of the four-person compliance consulting company) was not exactly what he would call 'fun.' When he'd started, he had worked with a lot of financial organizations, reading balance sheets and profit/loss statements and forms with identifiers like international phone numbers. Now he was working with hospitals and HMOs, matching their records and procedures against the laws passed in the last year and identifying problem areas.

At least he didn't have to talk to the customers, usually. He was happy enough to stand in the background at presentations and let his boss, a compact arctic fox, handle the client relations. Her name was Chantara, and she was really good at it.

They worked in an open office. The conference room was the only room with a door, and they only met in there when clients visited the office. This morning, when Fin walked in, Chantara lifted her head and shook it so that the four hoops in her ear jingled together.

"Morning, sunshine," she said, and laughed. "How we coming on the Sacred Heart 1421-790Ks?"

"Should have the eval done today." Fin was the new guy, the one Chantara and Jake had brought on two years ago when the workload had gotten big enough to warrant it. They appreciated Fin's reliability and didn't mind that he was quiet; Fin liked he could work without constant distractions without having to be alone in an office. Sometimes they all went out to lunch, and sometimes they all worked through lunch, and sometimes he and the other junior consultant Eileen went out, and sometimes he went by himself. They never forced him to be social, and as a result he was social more often.

He settled in to his desk to review the 1421-790K, the hospital's form for a doctor to request an exception to the usual process. They had to provide a reason, which could be anything from a patient allergy, to a shortage of the usual drug, to mysterious "singular circumstances." The compliance officer at Sacred Heart had explained wearily that this last bucket had expanded in the last two years to appear on nearly all of the forms filed, and that many doctors kept stacks of the exception form already filled out with "the doctor feels that singular circumstances require a variance to the usual procedure" as the explanation, to save time. This was causing the hospital a good deal of trouble with the insurance companies, and their client had requested specific attention to this form.

It was not fun, but it was engaging. Today, though, Fin kept finding his thoughts straying from the rows of text to the little laugh Amir gave when Fin joked about something. He wondered if Amir had read *Picnic*, as he'd said he would. Fin had downloaded an e-book on city planning, which was Amir's graduate program. The swift fox had found himself enjoying the history of it and was looking forward to talking to Amir and getting more detail on what he wanted to do with his degree.

4. When people ask how you are, say "Good" rather than "Okay." Even if you don't feel it.

He was deep into his analysis when Eileen walked in, humming. "How you doing, Fin?" she asked as she sat down at her desk.

"Good, good," he said. "You?"

"Dandy." She sat at her desk, started the computer, and then immediately got up for tea. Fin bent back to his work and never saw her come back.

It took him only a couple hours to finish the part of his work that required him to concentrate, and after that he was just typing up bland descriptions while his mind wandered. Whenever he found idiocies in a company's protocols, he always looked forward to sharing them with his theater buddies. Today, though, he found himself wondering if Amir would enjoy hearing some of them as well.

Sheesh, why was he thinking about the little fennec so much? He knew Hay wanted the two of them to hook up, and Amir doubtless knew it too. But Amir didn't seem to be in any more of a hurry than Fin was. He had his graduate courses to worry about, and Fin had his theater. They'd had coffee a couple times, and the conversation had come haltingly at first, but more easily the longer they talked. Now they had a standing once-a-week coffee break, on Thursdays when Amir's classes got out early.

But before Thursday of this week, there was the Hay date tonight. Fin waited until noon, when Hay would be on his lunch break, and excused himself to the conference room to make the call.

5. Do not talk about how you really feel.

"Darling," Hay said when Fin called him. "I was hoping you'd call."

"Oh?" Fin shifted the phone, looking out the window at the park. Snow covered the skeletons of the trees, covered the grass except along the paths where people hurried back and forth.

"Yes, I have sadly had something else come up. I hate to leave you at the last minute, but—"

Fin felt a stir of irritation. "Something else or someone else?"

"Fin." Hay's voice held a note of reproach. "If you want details, you know you have only to ask."

"All right. I'll call Amir."

"Already done, sweetie. He's meeting you tonight at The Gilded Leaf. Seven-thirty, don't be late."

Fin sighed and didn't say anything. He knew Hay was doing this on purpose to get him and Amir together. He stared at the park, where a lynx was struggling through the snow to get to her car. Hay said, "You're not mad at me, are you?"

"No." Fin closed his eyes. "It's fine. I'll call Amir."

"I told you, he's going to meet you."

"I know, I just want to confirm."

"You're not going to cancel." Hay's voice was firm.

"No," Fin said again. He opened his eyes. The lynx was brushing snow off her car, leaning desperately across the windshield. "I just want to confirm it's okay."

"All right. I'll catch up with you some other night, okay? Don't be mad at me, Fin dear."

"I'm not." The lynx slipped and fell into a snowdrift. She got up, struggling, and brushed snow from her coat. "I'll see you, Hay."

Fin put down the phone as the lynx finally got into her car. He waited to see if it would start. When the taillights blinked on, he dialed Amir.

"Hi," the fennec's high voice said. "Hay just called me. If you don't want to do The Gilded Leaf, that's okay."

Two wolves were hopping through the park now. The lynx's car drove away. Fin watched the wolves, a young couple who kept wagging their tails and playing in the snow. "I was actually thinking," he said. "You want to just wait 'til Hay's free?"

Amir didn't answer right away. Fin thought that perhaps he was trying not to be too relieved that Fin had suggested postponing. "No," Amir said. "I don't."

"You don't?"

"Let me put it this way." The fennec sounded more resolute, more serious than Fin had ever heard him. "If you don't want to get together tonight...just with me...then let's just cancel dinners."

6. Resist the urge to isolate yourself.

Cancel? Fin didn't have to think about it to know how he felt. But how would he say it? Could he bring himself to just blurt it out? How would he do it without sounding stupid?

"Fin?"

"Dinner, you mean? Just this dinner?" Fin said, scrabbling for something to say.

Amir's voice was a little quieter. "What do you think? Still want to get together?"

He could feel the fennec slipping away. If he thought of himself as a character in one of his plays, it was easier for him to say emotional things. "Yes," the character Fin blurted out. "I do. But..."

"But what?" Amir said, after a moment.

"Would you want to come over and have me cook you dinner?"

When Amir replied, his voice was light again. "I'd like that. I'd like that a lot."

Fin looked out into the park again. His tail was wagging. "Okay. Seven-thirty?"

"Perfect."

That single word echoed in Fin's head, warming him after the phone was hung up. He sat in the chair, tail wagging, and watched people walk through the park and play in the snow.

"You done in here?" Chantara said, knocking as she opened the door. "I need to call Sacred Heart. You can listen if you want. I'm just setting up our meeting for Friday."

"No, I'm done." Fin stood, taking one last look out at the park. A few more people were hurrying through the snow. He put his phone in his pocket and walked to the door as Chantara sat down at the table and dialed on the speakerphone. He closed the door behind him and sat down at his desk.

"You okay?" Eileen called over to him.

Fin shook his head and perked his ears up, realizing he'd been staring at his computer without touching anything. "I'm good," he said. He called up the next set of documents from Sacred Heart and started looking through them.

The doe kept looking at him. "I'm going to grab lunch from the deli. You want something?"

"No," Fin said, and then, "Actually, sure. Tuna salad?" He fished in his pocket for a ten.

"I thought you liked their barbecue chicken." Eileen got up and took the bill from him.

"I did, just sometimes it gives me indigestion."

She raised an eyebrow, looking down. "Maybe this time it won't."

He looked away from her, back at his screen. "Just the tuna salad."

"Whatever you want." She pulled her coat on and walked out.

Bridges

Amir's 'Perfect' stayed with Fin as he ate his sandwich, as he finished up his report, and as he started on his next project. When Chantara looked at his report and said, "This looks great," he heard Amir's 'Perfect' echoing behind it. The sensation was a little confusing, like the feeling of his tail wagging for no apparent reason, like the occasional moment when he would snap back to his reports and realize he hadn't been doing anything on them for the last five minutes.

Silly, stupid, and completely unlike him. If he sat and thought about it, he could hear the whispers that it wouldn't last, the trembling of the foundations beneath him. Sure, now that he and Amir hadn't talked for a while, Amir was happy to hang out with him, even looking forward to it. But after they'd had their date, after the conversation had gone on longer than their coffee talks and stalled or become awkward, after they'd attempted to have sex without the comfortable intermediary of Hayward, then what? Hayward had always left early, and Amir had never stayed the night, and even though the pills gave Fin the ability to tell himself that Amir still liked him, years of habit made it difficult for him to believe deep down inside.

7. Do something good for someone else.

Between the crowded, slushy parking lot and the long lines, it took forty-five minutes for Fin to do the shopping for the casserole and pick up cherry pie at the bakery down the street from his house. The casserole took an hour to bake, so he wanted it to go in around seven. Amir would arrive at seven-thirty, and they'd eat at eight.

Only it took him longer to pull all the meat off the chicken than he'd anticipated, and by the time he'd chopped all the celery, it was already seven. Hurriedly, he scooped the pieces into the casserole dish with the chicken and measured out the noodles and water, but it was still ten after seven before he got it in the oven.

That left him twenty minutes to stress over the fact that dinner would be a little later than he'd planned, until 7:31, when he snapped at himself to stop being an idiot. That freed him up to worry about why Amir was late, but fortunately, he only had to worry about that for five more minutes.

"Sorry I'm late," Amir said when Fin opened the door. They smiled at each other, hesitating on the edge of hugging, and then Fin leaned down to brush his muzzle to Amir's.

"Let me get that," he said as Amir shrugged out of his coat, but the fennec held on.

"I'll get it," he said, smiling. Beneath the coat he was wearing a short-sleeved silk shirt with red and gold patterns that hung loose over a pair of black jeans.

So Fin went to get wine while Amir was hanging up his coat in the closet. When Fin came out holding two glasses of wine, Amir was standing next to the couch. He looked deliberately down at the center cushion as Fin handed him the wine. There was a small grin on his muzzle. "No towel?"

Fin's ears flicked. "Well, Hay isn't here," he said.

Amir's ears lowered. The grin faded, and he looked uncertain. "Yeah..."

Fin cleared his throat. "Thanks for coming anyway. I wanted to try this casserole recipe. I haven't cooked in a while."

"It smells great." Amir sipped the wine. "This is nice. As usual." He sat down in what was becoming his customary corner of the couch.

"If nothing else, my folks gave me good taste in wine." Fin took a seat in the opposite corner.

Amir cocked his head. "You drank wine with your parents?"

"Yeah." Fin's tail swished slowly. He looked down into his glass. "I was drinking wine with dinner from the time I was ten."

"I didn't have a drink until I was twenty-two." Amir smiled. "I would go to bars and order a Coke in a small glass, so people thought I had rum in it."

"Didn't your friends take you out on your twenty-first?"

The fennec shook his head. "I didn't have the kind of friends you drink with. Or, really, many friends." He laughed shortly. "I didn't say that to sound pathetic. I just don't make friends easily."

"I know how that is." Fin sipped at his drink.

The silence after that remark stretched on. "So," Amir said. "How's the play going?"

And Fin told him about the rehearsals, about the continuing struggle to coax a passable performance out of Charisse, about his own excitement over his role. "It's just a supporting part, but I'm getting into it. I'm the rich guy that the older girl is going to marry. Where everyone else is making rash decisions about dating and running off together, I'm more logical. The lead character is an old college friend of mine who rushes into things without thinking. I have a song with him called 'Look Before You Sleep.'"

Amir laughed again. Fin smiled and sang, "Look before you sleep / with the first girl on the dance floor / There's no hurry; keep / on looking 'til you're real sure ..."

"That's nice." Amir leaned toward Fin, his ears straight up. "I don't think you ever sang for me before. You have a really nice voice."

"It's just a normal baritone." But Fin's tail wagged against the couch at the compliment.

"I can't really sing," Amir said. "I used to play violin in high school. Just got bored of it."

"You know, if you're not in love with music, it becomes more of a chore..." Fin looked down at his wine. "There are a lot of things I gave up after high school."

"Like what?"

Fin flicked his ears. "Girls."

He'd said it secretly hoping to hear Amir's laugh again, and the fennec did not disappoint him. "Oh, I gave those up after middle school. I mean, I had a lot of good friends who were girls. We went shopping together."

"You keep in touch with any of them?"

"Some." Amir finished his wine. "They don't travel all that much. We chat online every now and then. But it's not the same as having someone to hang out with, you know."

Fin nodded. He inhaled the sharp aroma of the wine, letting the sting of the alcohol fade so he could smell the fruit undertones. He lapped again and let the flavors roll over his tongue. "No, it's not," he said.

Before the ensuing silence could turn awkward, the oven timer beeped. Fin got up and set his wine glass down. "I'll just..."

Amir had looked up at the beeping, and now was looking back down at his glass. His ears had lowered somewhat. He was clearly still thinking about his last remark. Fin stayed standing where he was until Amir's muzzle lifted and the fennec smiled at him. "Going to get that?"

The beeping did not get any softer, but it faded in his perception. "I'm glad you're here," the character Fin said with a returning smile.

Amir's ears came up. His smile broadened. "I'm glad too," he said. "Do you need help with dinner?"

8. Exercise.

"At least let me help with the cleanup." Amir licked his lips. "You did all the cooking and it was really good."

"You don't need to keep saying that." Fin wagged his tail. "There's not much to clean up. I just throw stuff in the dishwasher."

He did so with a little more haste than usual, while Amir continued their dinner conversation, telling Fin about the land use class he was taking. Fin put on some water to boil for tea, interrupting Amir to ask if chai was okay.

"Sure." Amir's tail swung back and forth. He watched Fin take out two mugs, two tea pouches, and a container of chai tea.

"This'll take a little while." Fin gestured for Amir to return to the living room, and followed the fennec back to the couch. When Fin sat in his corner, though, Amir sat closer, in the middle. That was hopeful. Fin hadn't been sure Amir would want to do anything intimate without Hayward. Even though they'd seen each other naked three times now, even though they'd seen each other climax, they hadn't actually touched each other. Not unless you counted them being inside the same fox at the same time, which Fin didn't.

So it was a little awkward without a red fox between them. They didn't put on any movies, which Hayward would have insisted on. Fin played an old musical soundtrack for background, and just tried to be interesting enough that Amir wouldn't want to leave. Whether it was through his efforts or not, the fennec seemed perfectly happy to talk about his land use class, and the city planning book Fin had started reading. Then Amir was happy to listen to a story about one of Fin's customers from last year, and that led to a lively discussion about the bookstores in Gateway and whether the selection of books was more important than whether the bookstore catered to canids and their sensitive noses.

In the course of that discussion, Amir leaned forward, gesturing to make a point. Fin was just responding when the fennec seemed to slip, falling forward and just catching himself with a paw on Fin's leg, his muzzle inches from the swift fox's.

Fin's words died away. He looked into Amir's eyes, saw the hesitant smile, and returned it. Slowly, he set his wine glass down on the coffee table. Amir's paw firmed its grip on Fin's thigh. "Is this okay?" the fennec said softly.

"Yeah." Fin wanted to say how glad he was that the fennec had made the first move, but that seemed silly. He reached up and brushed a paw down Amir's arm, from the elbow to the wrist, his blunt claws parting the soft desert fur. For the first time, it occurred to him how odd it was that the fennec had worn short sleeves, even with his thick winter coat. Then he understood why Amir had done it, that he had made the first move before even stepping into the apartment, and Fin had been too dense to notice it.

"It's just weird without Hayward here." Amir's tail flicked at Fin's touch. "I mean, I'm glad...but we haven't really..."

"No." Fin leaned forward to touch his nose to the fennec's. "It is a little weird. I mean, we've seen each other..."

"Yeah." Amir's ears flattened, though he was smiling. He kissed Fin's nose lightly. "And you're...uh. Pretty hot."

I don't really get into physical looks, Fin wanted to tell him. I don't care whether someone's hot or not. But he couldn't make those words sound like anything other than a polite way of saying, I'm willing to sleep with you even though you're not that hot. So he just said, "You're pretty great to look at, too," which felt truthful and an acceptable compromise. Then he added, "That's a great shirt."

Amir leaned a little closer. "I kinda...want to see you again. If you're okay with it." He teased a claw beneath Fin's vest, pushing it further open. "Without the shirt."

Fin almost laughed, that Amir was just as worried as he was. "I'm okay," he said.

"Because you didn't put a towel down." Amir rubbed the sofa cushion. "I wondered."

"Well." Fin reached up to the fennec's side. It wasn't so hard to do this, not so hard as he'd thought it would be. Partly it was that Amir had made the first move, twice. Partly it was him telling himself that he wanted this, pushing aside the doubts and worries that always dragged him down. But partly, too, it was that the doubts and worries were faded, weaker. Amir had stayed through dinner, Amir was leaning in close to him, the cute, sexy fennec wanted to make love. Fin could smell that as clearly as the residual smell of the chicken casserole. He curled his paw around Amir's ribs and pulled the smaller fox down against him. "It seemed forward."

Amir came toward him eagerly, his chest against Fin's, his muzzle brushing the swift fox's. "Without Hayward."

Fin nodded. The fennec's weight felt good against him, comfortable and safe. He put himself into the character of Fin again, determined to make up for missing the clue of the silk shirt. "Also," he said, "I thought you might like to see the bedroom."

Amir wriggled out of his clothes like a snake while Fin was still unbuttoning his shirt. The fennec lay on the bed, tail thwapping the sheets, already halfway out of his sheath and getting more erect as he watched Fin undress. "You're fast," Fin said. He'd seen Amir before, but always over Hayward's shoulder, over Hayward's back. Never alone, never just for him.

"At some things." Amir smiled. "It's kinda cool watching you like this. Without Hayward, I mean."

Fin dropped his clothes in the hamper and wriggled slowly, starting out being the character Fin undressing for his lover. He pushed his boxers over his own growing erection and dropped them atop his slacks in the hamper, then turned to the bed.

The moment dragged on. Amir's tail thumped the bed a couple times and then stopped. His eyes met Fin's, a little bit of uncertainty in them. Fin felt it too; his own tail twitched. He tried to banish the specter of the red fox between them. After all, he told himself, Hayward only brought them on dates to bring them to this moment. He had confidence that they would be good together.

It wasn't Hay that was important, though. It was Amir. Fin knew, just knew, that the fennec was hesitating because he felt he'd already pushed to have this date, that he was waiting for Fin. And Fin did want him, with his mind and his heart as well as the heat between his legs. He'd already made the decision, so all he had to do was act on it. He took a step forward and saw Amir's eyes light up. From there, it was easy for him to get up on the bed, kneeling facing the fennec.

The fennec looked up at him and then rolled up to his knees, his smile wide. "Hi there, hotness," he said softly. He brought a paw up between Fin's legs, cupping his sac, and kept it there as he lowered his muzzle. His small tongue lapped at the swift fox's erect shaft, sliding gently up the length and along the tip, making Fin inhale and close his eyes.

"Hay really should have left us alone before," Fin said, reaching a paw down to cup Amir's cheekruff.

"He did." Amir pressed his nose into Fin's hip and inhaled, then breathed out slowly. "Just we were all worn out by then."

"Uh-huh." Fin lifted his muzzle as Amir's tongue washed up his shaft again, curling around the tip. "You don't seem worn out now."

"Uh-uh." Amir moved his paw around to Fin's rear, cupping it and holding it as he licked. "I'm...full of energy."

Fin arched his back, lowering his muzzle and opening his eyes. Amir's dusty-furred muzzle was moving up and down in warm, tingling waves, and the fennec's eyes were half-closed. His tail swung back and forth. Fin didn't feel the urge to say anything more, not then, not when Amir tugged his shaft forward, not when Amir's muzzle slid down over Fin's length, not even when the fennec's warm tongue and lips made Fin's shaft tremble, made his toes and tail curl, made him gasp out loud.

It wasn't until Amir had lifted his muzzle off that Fin spoke. His fingers were pressed into the fennec's cheek fur still, but as Amir leaned back, Fin loosened his fingers and rubbed through the thick, soft fur. "You're good at that," he said. "Better than Hay."

Amir giggled, and gave Fin's shaft another lick. "You're just saying that. I can't believe it."

"Hay's pretty good," Fin admitted. "But you feel different."

"I'd hope so." Amir's large ears flicked backwards. "You taste good."

Fin dropped to a crouch, touched his nose to Amir's, and pushed the fennec backwards onto the bed. What would the character Fin say? Ah. "Let's see how you taste."

The words came easily, and brought another smile from Amir as he lay back, letting his erection flop onto his ivory white belly fur. Fin took the base of it and tilted it upwards, lowering his muzzle at the same time. He breathed in Amir's thick musk, and lowered his tongue.

Hay was big, but Fin had never had the red fox in his muzzle. Amir felt almost as big, certainly bigger than anyone else Fin had ever put his lips around. He didn't have a lot of experience, but he knew he'd never worried about getting a sore jaw with any of the others. He didn't remember any of the others wriggling and moaning breathily quite so delightedly, either. Amir's whole body twitched, his paws clenching around the sheets, and when Fin rubbed his tongue hard along Amir's tip, the fennec actually squealed.

Fin was smiling when he looked up Amir's fluffy chest, letting the fennec's large shaft drop gently to his stomach. The fennec was staring up at the ceiling, but tilted his head downward. "You're pretty good, too," he gasped.

"Nah." Fin shook his head. "I, uh, need more practice."

He winced. That wasn't something the character Fin would say. It was goofy and kind of self-deprecating and kind of forward. But Amir curled his tail around so it brushed Fin's chest, and said, softly, "You can practice on me whenever you want."

That was goofy and forward too, and it made Fin smile, brought a warmth to his chest that matched the one between his legs. He rested a paw on Amir's stomach, feeling the warmth underneath. His claws ruffled the fur. "So," he said. "Um. You looked pretty good last time."

Amir flicked his ears. "I think anyone would look good behind Hayward."

"Yeah, well." Fin rubbed, pushing his paw up and back down. "If you want to, um. I don't need to top."

"Oh. Okay." Amir brought his paw to Fin's wrist. "I'd...like that, yeah."

Impulsively, Fin dropped to Amir's side and pulled the fennec against him. "Mmm," he said. "Well, okay then."

Amir draped an arm over Fin and ruffled the fur down his spine, around the base of his tail. He smoothed fur over the curve of Fin's rear. "We don't have to do that all the time."

"Let's worry about next time when it happens." Fin's tail thumped the bed.

Amir's claws teased down under his tail, brushing his tailhole there. "Sounds okay with me."

They held each other a little while longer, paws teasing between each other's legs, until Fin couldn't wait any longer. He kissed Amir's nose, said, "Be right back," and ran to the bathroom.

He brought a condom and a towel back with the lube, the little bottle already open as he got back to the bed. He rubbed the slick jelly under his wagging tail while Amir unrolled the condom down over his shaft. "Can I have a little of that?" Amir asked, his latex-covered shaft bobbing ready between his legs.

"Of course." Fin squirted more into his paw, but instead of moving to Amir's held-out paw, he wrapped his paw around Amir's shaft and slid it up and down, gripping the small swell of Amir's growing knot at the base. The fennec squirmed, spreading his legs and closing his eyes. When he started shuddering, Fin slid his paw free. "Okay, I think you're slick enough now."

Amir cracked one eye open. "Are you sure?"

"Pretty sure." Fin eyed Amir's knot, wondering how much bigger it would get. But he wanted it, he knew that, so he lay back on the towel, spreading his own legs and curling his tail to one side.

The fennec rubbed a paw along Fin's stomach, down the ivory fur and over into the brown fur of his hips. "I've, uh..." He let his fingers glide over Fin's erection and slight knot, down to his sheath and sac. "I mean, I've only ever done it from the back."

Fin turned toward Amir. "We can do it that way, too. If you want."

"I've seen pictures, just never, y'know." His paw closed around Fin's shaft. "But I'm up for trying."

Fin reached out to stroke Amir's hardness with his slick paw. "Clearly." He smiled. "Just kneel between my legs, like this..." He guided Amir to the right position and lifted his hips, tightening his stomach and resting his feet on Amir's thighs. "And I think you can figure it out from here?"

Amir arched his eyebrows and nodded, leaning forward. The tip of his erection pressed under Fin's tail. The fennec looked down, panting, and stopped. "You okay?"

"Yeah." Fin wrapped his legs around Amir's waist and pulled the fennec in closer. He forced his muscles to relax as Amir, taking the hint, pressed his hips forward. The pressure of the fennec's shaft increased until it slid inside Fin with a warm, familiar intimacy.

It had been a while. The only sex he'd had lately had been with Hayward, and Hay never let anyone else bottom. The mild soreness went away almost immediately, replaced with a warm glow rippling through his rear. Fin arched his back and held Amir's wrist with his dry paw, while the slicker one rested on his shaft. "Still okay?" Amir asked.

"Yes." Fin squeezed with his legs, tugging Amir closer, and the fennec took the hint. Fin relaxed as the wide shaft drove further in, all the way up to the swell of the knot, and then pressing that inside, until the fennec's muzzle was just over Fin's chest. Amir was biting his lip and his body was trembling again. Fin squeezed his wrist until the brown eyes met his, and he smiled. "Feels good," he said.

"Uh-huh." Amir gasped. He pulled out and then thrust back in, good and quick, and Fin started stroking himself so Amir could just focus on fucking him. Because the dusty-yellow muzzle had lifted, the brown eyes

now unfocused, and he was thrusting harder. His whole body felt taut and quivering against Fin.

The swift fox was getting pretty close himself, but not quite that close. He slid his paw along his shaft faster, trying to catch up. He angled his hips up, with a little more tightening of his stomach, and that helped; the back-and-forth of Amir's shaft became more electric, the press of his growing knot a spike of pleasure each time it pushed its way in past Fin's muscles.

The fennec was gasping, thrusting, his paws gripping Fin's chest fur. Fin closed his eyes to focus, but he still didn't beat Amir to the climax. With a high-pitched moan, Amir thrust all the way into Fin, his knot full and tight, his hips jerking, and the clutch of his fingers was almost painful. Fin kept his legs wrapped around the slender waist, his own arousal surging with each shudder of the small fennec above him and inside him. He watched the muzzle hanging open, perked his ears to the yelps, so familiar and yet different this time. He could not only hear them, but he could feel them in the warmth of Amir's paws, in the sliding thrusts inside him.

Amir's paws slid down around Fin's chest; his body sagged against the swift fox's taut stomach, moving with the rising and falling of Fin's panting. Fin's own hips squirmed, his knot tight and hard below his strokes. He clenched around Amir's shaft and knot, feeling every inch of it and eliciting another squeak from the fennec, his climax approaching, building. It crested slowly, as his paw moved faster, until his back was arching up all the way into Amir's stomach. The warmth spread outward from his groin, making his fingers and toes and tail tingle, and then he let out his own moan as the pleasure exploded through him, spattering his stomach with each jerk of his paw. He gasped, stroking until the pleasure subsided, and then collapsed on the bed.

The fennec fell on top of him, still pressed securely inside. Fin wrapped his free arm around Amir's back, keeping the other tight around his still-pulsing erection. Amir's arms dug into the bed under Fin's shoulders, pulling him close.

They lay together, panting, tails brushing past each other. Amir's weight felt nice on Fin's stomach, and though his shaft was getting a bit uncomfortable inside Fin's rear now, pulling that big knot out would've been worse. He just relaxed and focused on the smell of Amir, the sound of his panting, the wiry body in his arms. And the discomfort faded away, like his worries and doubts. His body felt pleasantly tired, and Amir's presence around him was soothing.

9. Commend yourself for something you did well today.

"Can I stay here?" Amir murmured next to Fin's ear.

"Sure." Fin squeezed him. "You can stay as long as you want."

"I have to go to class," Amir said. "At ten. But until then."

"I leave for work at eight."

"Mm-kay." Amir nuzzled Fin's cheek. "That was really good. Really good."

"Yeah." Fin rubbed his muzzle back, his tail wagging. "You feel wonderful."

"Who needs Hayward, huh?"

Fin laughed, bouncing Amir on his chest. "Aw, don't be mean. He did introduce us."

"I'm not being mean. I just mean...I don't think we need him to go on dates any more. I'd like to start seeing you. Just you."

A different kind of warmth spread through Fin, from Amir's warm fur down to the black tip of Fin's tail. It felt like going on his first Hay date and having a good time, like moving to Gateway by himself and getting a good apartment and job, like picking exactly the right gift for his boyfriend in college, like all of that rolled into one and then multiplied. He closed his eyes and pressed his nose into Amir's fur, between the large ears. "Mmm. Me too."

10. Tomorrow will be a good day.

The calendar said summer was almost here, but only in the last week had the warm, moist air of spring allowed Carmila to open the windows. She smelled flowers from the trees outside and the mingled scents of the people who walked by, and though she'd be tired of the crowds by the end of summer, for now they made her feel less isolated. Even though the nighttime air was cooler, the freshness was worth it.

Not that she felt as alone this spring as she had the last three years. The white carnations on her desk, the first fresh flowers she'd had in her room in years, didn't smell as strongly as the flowers outside, but the scent and their white brilliance reminded her that she wasn't alone—at the times when she couldn't see Pinzer on instant messenger.

She'd long since gotten past the awkwardness of getting her personal interactions on the computer. Right now, she was reading practice questions for the bar exam, scrolling down with one paw while the other paw cupped her breast inside the open collared shirt. She tweaked her nipple with a claw, trying to keep her arousal level up while waiting for Pinzer to reply to her latest message. Multiple choice legal questions were not so good for that, but she had to get through this one if she was going to take the bar in two weeks. She glanced at the time on the laptop. Quarter past one, which meant Hayward would be home soon.

She flipped back to the IM window and stared at her last message:

> Carmila2009 grasps your ready shaft and guides it into her, gasping as you enter her. Her paws move around your hips, pulling you insied her.

The typo bothered her, but that was the price of typing quickly. She went back to the practice questions. If Pinzer didn't come back in another ten minutes, he was going to have a severe case of coitus interruptus.

The IM window flashed. She flipped back to it.

> PinzColler smiles, his nose brushing yours. "Someone's eager," he gasps. He thrusts in, his length filling you, and then he applies his

tongue to your other nipple, washing
over it.

Finally.

Carmila2009 throws her head back
and takes in a shuddering breathe.
"Someone has a roommate coming home
soon," she pants, pulling your body
cloes. "So get both paws on the
keys."

PinzColler smirks. "That's no
fun." He starts a nice rhythm, in
and out, not neglecting your breasts,
his claws stroking the fur as he
nibbles. "I'm sure Hayward wouldn't
mind."

God, it was irritating how he never made a typo. But it was also hot.

Carmila2009 brings her head forward
to bite your ear gently. "I mind,"
she says, pushing her hips forward
to meet yours. "And mentioning him
is killing the mood."

Which wasn't strictly true. She switched paws so she could work the
other breast, imagining it was Pinz's paw and not hers, imagining him
actually inside her. Imagining she could feel it. The memory was strong
enough to complement her fingers circling her nipples and get her body
flush. The smell of her arousal drifted up to her, exciting her further. She
glanced at the bottle of wine and the nearly-empty glass next to it, but
she was already warm enough inside.

If only Hayward regularly drove, she could listen for his car pulling
up. But he got rides with friends, or, when it was warm enough, walked.
So the only warning she had of his arrival was often the key in the door.
She'd been careful thus far with Pinz, though their sessions were going
later and later, and it was only because it was a Thursday night that she'd
let it go this late.

He was taking forever again. He didn't multi-task as well as she did.
Which meant either he was working on his practice essays, or he had
gotten a little too into their session.

```
Carmila2009 grinds against you,
moaning as she feels your thick, hot
length insied her, its warmth filling
her cunny with ripples of pleasure.
She rubs her leg along yours, inhaling
your scent adn biting your ear a
little more sharply.
```

If he wasn't going to respond to that, then she'd just finish herself, too. But Pinz was pretty good about knowing when to respond, and sure enough, his reply flashed up a moment later.

```
PinzColler drives deep inside you,
moans of pleasure vibrating through
your breasts. He pumps faster as
you bite his ear, his tail arching
behind him. "Nnnf, Carm," he pants,
shuddering, his fur pressed to yours
as his hips work faster and faster.
```

At least she could note that he used 'faster' three times in that one. So he had been jerking off. Meant he was probably pretty close now.

```
Carmila2009 whines, your ear held
between her teeth as her body heat
rises, legs wrapping around yoru
hips to
```

Noises outside the door. A moment later, the key turned. She hit the enter key in a panic, hid the chat window, and poured another glass of wine with a shaking paw.

Hayward hummed a tune, opening the door. "Up late studying?" he said as it closed.

"Up late fucking?" She took a drink of wine, fighting resentment. The shivering of her body, still craving release, wasn't his fault. Nor was the guilt that flushed her ears and the back of her neck. It was hers, all hers.

Behind her, the red fox hummed, getting closer. She checked her screen again to make sure the chat window was hidden, edged her wheelchair closer to the desk, and picked up the wine just as Hayward came up behind her. She flicked her ears as he kissed between them. Warmth spread from that brief touch, and now her arousal was almost

completely submerged by guilt and regret. Hayward probably wouldn't have smelled it even if she hadn't been masking it with the strong scent of the wine glass she held to her muzzle until he straightened.

"Actually," he said, "I was out with Kinzi again. I brought Jock along, but he and Kinzi started arguing about movies. Jock got kind of offended and the mood wasn't right, so I broke it off. Oh, you got flowers." He inhaled the carnations' delicate scent and smiled. "They look nice. What's the occasion?"

The card from Pinz was safely hidden in the pocket of her shirt. "Just felt like brightening up the room. Jock's the platypus?" She sipped from the wine. Its tang steadied her. She took another sip and then put the glass down.

Hay snorted softly. "I don't know any platypusses. Platypi? Jock's a cougar. He's a dancer, really social, but he's got this sweet romantic streak. I thought he'd be okay. But Kinzi just didn't seem to like him."

"Cougar." Carmila felt her composure return. "Not the one who stuck his paw down your pants at the rave last week? Cause *he* sounded like a catch."

"That was Axel, and he does not need to be set up. Jock's the one I met through Boris at their dinner two weeks ago. Honestly, he wasn't good enough for Kinzi, but I was running out of ideas. I don't know who else to bring along with Kinzi now. He needs someone really special."

Carmila tried to focus on her practice questions. "Just go out with him yourself already. He must like you, at least."

He laughed, padded back to the kitchen, and poured himself a drink. "Want anything?"

"I'm serious."

"About what?" She could hear him in the kitchen doorway, drinking.

"You've been seeing this coyote for what, half a year?"

"Sometimes it takes that long." He drank again. "Took me a year and a half to get Fin set up with Amir."

"So why not date this coyote yourself?"

She heard the clink of his empty glass on the kitchen counter. He wandered back over to her. "Don't stay up too late. Past a certain time, you don't retain information anymore."

"*I'm* fine." She had read the same question three times now, still with no idea what it said.

"You're doing great focusing on the questions. You haven't talked about random cases in months." He yawned. "You'll pass the bar, no problem."

The IM window flashed. She looked away from it. "It's good to have something else to focus on. The bar exam, I mean."

"Oh, I got the day off, so I can take you down there. You don't need to get a ride with Tonio."

Tell him. Tell him now. "He's going anyway, so…"

"This'll be easier. I've got the space in the back for the chair. Besides, I want to be there with you."

She squeezed her eyes shut. "Hay…"

He rested a paw on her shoulder. "Sorry. I'll let you study."

She could smell booze and musk, with his hips right at her nose level. He'd gone to a bar after dinner, probably, but it didn't smell like he'd picked anyone up. Just cruising for lonely hearts, desperate souls he could tell her about. "G'night," she said.

When his paw finally lifted from her shoulder, he brushed her cheekruff very lightly. He had the same delicate touch that Foster had, but the echo was muted now, her body still aching for Pinzer's imaginary touch.

He closed the bedroom door behind him. She heard the creak as he climbed up to his bunk and settled in, and then was still.

She brought the chat window back.

> PinzColler grins. "Someone come home?"

> Carmila2009 nods. "Sorry."

> PinzColler kisses your nose. "S'okay, sweetie. I waited for you." He wraps his arms around you. "I'm looking forward to meeting him. He sounds like an interesting guy."

> Carmila2009 nuzzles back. "He is."

She reached inside her shirt and caressed her breast again, but the arousal was mostly gone. She sighed. She would go through the motions for Pinz, and then go to sleep. And she would tell Hay in the morning.

But when she cracked her eyes open, he was already drying his fur from the shower, humming softly. She didn't want to tell him from the bed, because then she'd be trapped there. The last few years had taught her to cope with the helplessness she felt in bed, away from her chair, but it lurked in the back of her mind. Without Pinz to distract her, her thoughts turned backwards darkly, each little twinge in her shoulders a reminder of that night. No, from bed was not a time to have any meaningful discussions.

So she lay back, and when he came in buttoning his dress shirt over his boxers and said, "Need anything this morning?" she just shook her head.

He smiled and pulled on a pair of slacks. "I'm going to Fin's play after work, and then there'll be an after party, and Fin said something about going out after that. Don't know when I'll be home."

"Hay," she said. He flicked his ears to focus on her. "Could we go out for lunch tomorrow?"

He reached for a belt. "Sure. Where do you want to go?"

Doesn't matter, she almost said, and then realized that would tip him off that it was more than just a lunch. She started to say, "Fairmont Diner," until she remembered that that place came to mind because it had been one of Foster's favorites to take her, and later Hay. "Angelica's."

"Mmm. Monte Cristo sandwiches. It's a date." His bright smile as he left made her feel positively depressed.

She didn't get out of bed for another hour, though she was painfully aware of how unprepared she felt for the bar. Pinz was practicing essays full time and she was still obsessively going through practice multiple choice tests four or five hours a day. Finally, her empty stomach drove her from the warmth of the bed to the chair, the shower, the kitchen, and back to the desk, where she held out for only forty-five minutes before connecting to see if Pinz was on.

He was, working on essays, of course. They kept up a light conversation about the bar exams before he brought up again the subject of his visit.

> PinzColler: How much did you tell
> Hayward about me?

> Carmila2009 told him all he needed
> to know.

> PinzColler grins. "Like what?"

She sat and stared at the screen. It was such a lawyer thing to do, to meet her evasive response with a gentle prod for more specifics. When she realized it had been two minutes since he'd asked, she knew with cold certainty what was coming next, and sure enough, within thirty seconds of her realization, he sent another message.

> PinzColler: Did you tell him, sweetie?

> Carmila2009 sighs.

> PinzColler sighs. "I know it's hard for you, but you have to tell him before I show up there. Unless you want me to spirit you away in the dead of night so the poor boy will wake up to an empty apartment."

> Carmila2009: No.

> Carmila2009: I'm going to do it tomorrow.

> PinzColler hugs you. "It's going to hurt him. There's nothing you can do about that except make it as gentle and loving as possible."

That would be hard enough, but she could do it, because she knew it was the best thing for him, even though it was going to hurt. The hurt would be hard, but she could bear it. The hurt wasn't the worst part. She couldn't tell Pinz the worst part, not over the computer. She felt she could tell him anything. But she would have to tell him to his face, so that she could see immediately that he didn't hate her.

> Carmila2009: I know. It's just... he's gonna be all happy for me, and he'll ask me embarrassing things like what's your cock size, and I don't want to have to deal with all that.

> PinzColler: What are you going to tell him?

> Carmila2009: Just that we met online, that we want a lot of the

Bridges

same things, that I need to move on and make a new life.

PinzColler: No, I mean about my cock size.

Carmila2009: I'll think of something.

Carmila2009: If you want to get in on a three-way with him, I can have him set something up for next week.

PinzColler will not deny that he's intrigued, but presumes it would probably have some emotional component, and so he'd better not.

PinzColler: Have you ever watched?

Carmila2009: Oh God.

PinzColler: I didn't think so, but you never know. Some brothers and sisters share a lot. :)

Carmila2009 reminds you that we're not legally brother and sister.

PinzColler: Everything but, though.

Carmila2009: Funny, I'm sure I hhave a few essays here about 'legal' being a big deal.

PinzColler: Isn't the purpose of the law to codify those relationships that exist as a function of people living together in society? There are verbal binding contracts and common law marriages.

```
     Carmila2009:    We've    only    been
living together four years. We're not
common-law married. Anyway, I could
get a divorce real easily. Three
quarters of the gay men in this town
would testify to that.

     PinzColler arches an eyebrow. "You
either have a small town or a very
active brother."

     Carmila2009: You can ask him when
you meet him. He'll be happy to tell
yuo.

     PinzColler: Tell him tomorrow.

     Carmila2009: I promise.

     Carmila2009: Bearish.

     PinzColler: ?

     Carmila2009:    "Bearish."    That's
what I'll tell him.

     PinzColler checks his pants. "I
fear I may disappoint you, darling."
: (
```

Carmila grinned and had to hug herself. Pinz never failed to make her feel whole, whether it was his easy, comfortable respect for her or his sweet little names for her. It didn't make her other worries go away, but it put them in perspective.

```
Carmila2009: Never.
```

If things went well, she and Pinz would be together for a long time. And Hayward would get over her leaving. Eventually. She went back to her essays, forcing herself to focus.

Though she'd had a late breakfast, it had been only a granola bar, so a couple hours later, she was thinking about lunch when the land line rang. She and Hayward both had cell phones, so the only people to call the land line were telemarketers and her school. She let the machine pick it up, perking an ear. Hayward had recorded the message, because he was away so often and she was afraid someone might hear her voice on the machine and know there was a wheelchair-bound vixen alone in the apartment. That had been a long time ago; she wasn't as worried now, but it wasn't worth re-recording it.

When the speaker clicked over, there was a brief moment of silence. Telemarketing machine, she thought, and reached for the remote extension to hang up. Her finger had just found the button when a very non-machine-like voice spoke.

"Hay, it's Kinzi. Listen, I didn't want to bother you at work."

Carmila turned to stare at the phone, both ears perked now. He had a mature, calm voice, fairly deep. "Just wanted to apologize about last night."

Wheels turned in her mind, connections forming. A possibility, a way out that just might work, that might save her the reality of the pain she was already anticipating. Kinzi went on: "It was a dumb argument and...I dunno, I'm sorry, swishy. Don't give up on me, okay? See you soon."

She had to try it. The speakerphone button was right next to the disconnect button. She shifted her finger and tapped it. "Hello?"

For a moment, she thought he'd hung up. "Kinzi?" she said.

"Hello?" He sounded guarded. As guarded, she supposed, as if he'd called a friend and a stranger had answered.

"I'm sorry," she said. "I'm Carmila. I live with Hayward."

"Oh. He never told me..."

She could hear him thinking, so that's why we never went back to his place. "He doesn't talk about me very much." Now that she'd introduced herself, she was at a loss to explain the impulse that had led her to talk to Kinzi. All she knew was that her joking comment to Hayward from the previous night was still in the back of her head, and that the affection in Kinzi's voice had given her the desperate hope that had impelled her to act.

"Are you a convicted felon under house arrest?"

She smiled. "If only it were that romantic. I'm his sister."

"I...thought he was an only child."

"In a manner of speaking. I'm more of a sister in law, except not in law."

Now there was a longer pause. "If he doesn't have a brother...that means you do."

She could hear him trying to keep his tone neutral. She made the same effort. "I did," she said.

"Oh." His voice softened. "Oh, I'm sorry."

"How long have you known Hay?"

"About eight months now, I guess. We met at that party at Boris's place in November." He paused. "You're not like a recluse or anything, are you?"

"I'm a cripple."

"I'm sorry." He barked a short laugh. "Sorry, I mean, for apologizing all the time. I know you must get that a lot. Seems like you've had a rough time."

"I'm fine." She grinned to herself. "Listen, can I ask you a favor?"

"Sure?"

"I don't get out of the house too often. And I hate eating alone. I know you don't know me, but we both know Hayward pretty well." Hopefully the hook of knowing Hayward would reel him in.

He didn't answer immediately. "I'm a little busy."

"You're not working right now."

"I could be on a break."

"I can hear the espresso machine in the background. So unless you work at a coffee shop..."

"I have other plans for lunch."

To her almost-attorney's ear, it didn't sound believable. "I'll explain about me and Hayward."

"Really, I—"

"And my brother."

From the silence, she knew he would say yes. Still, he hesitated. "Did you pick up the phone just to have company for lunch?"

"No," she said. "Hayward's talked about you."

His tone turned to amused resignation. "Where do you want to meet?"

She copied his number from the caller ID, just in case, and wheeled herself down to The Sandwich Wizard, a sit-down lunch place a few blocks away. The sun felt nice on her fur, and people held doors for her, so she was still in a good mood when the coyote walked into the restaurant. She knew him right away, though she couldn't have said how: he just had that mature look that matched his voice. When he looked around, she waved at him, and he didn't look startled to see an arctic fox; he just smiled and walked over to her table to join her.

The chubby skunk who was waiting on them came over immediately with a menu. "Iced tea," Kinzi said absently, scanning the sandwiches. "Any recommendations?" he asked, when the skunk had left.

"The tuna fish is excellent. If you like bits of apple and dill."

"Love it. Sounds like a winner." He put the menu down and looked across the table at her over his wire-rimmed glasses. He was dressed in a business casual shirt, open at the collar, and a gold pen was stuck in his shirt pocket. "So."

His eyes flicked around, taking in her features while his ears stayed steady. She took a breath. "Foster was my older brother. He was killed in a car accident a little over four years ago." Her paw rested on the wheelchair arm. She tried to think how long it had been since she'd said those words.

"You were in the crash." She nodded. "And Hayward was..."

"His boyfriend. Partner." She held up two fingers. "Two years."

Kinzi exhaled, his fur creasing between his eyebrows. "I'm sorry."

"It's okay." She could hear Pinz's voice saying the next words an instant before she did. "It's been a long time. He wouldn't want me to be sad."

"So you were living with him and Hayward?"

She shook her head. "After the accident, I tried living with my parents, but they're not really handicapped-accessible. Their house, I mean. So I got an apartment and Hay...came to take care of me."

He looked away from her. "For four years."

"Too long." she said. "I know."

He drummed his fingers on the table top. "Why did you pick up the phone?"

The change of subject helped her clear her head. "Hay's talked about you. I wanted to talk to you."

"He really talks about me?"

"Oh yes. Though I don't think he realizes how hung up you are on him. Which is funny, because Hay's usually pretty good about that sort of thing." His eyes widened, his carefully controlled expression gone as his ears flattened. He opened his muzzle to protest, but she didn't let him get a word in. "It was that way with Foster, too, at least as far as I remember. He came home talking about this gorgeous red fox who liked him as a friend and a flirt but didn't seem to take a hint."

"I'm not...why do you think..." Kinzi cleared his throat. "I appreciate all Hay's efforts to get me over Jake and find someone else. I'm just very picky, is all."

"Mm." She sipped her Coke while the waiter returned with the iced tea. He took their sandwich order and left again immediately. "That's why you pick stupid fights with the boys he brings on your dates. Four of them now, I think? That's why you make a special phone call to say, 'don't give up on me,' right?"

He frowned. "I was just being friendly. He goes to a lot of trouble to find people he thinks I'll like, and I don't want to seem ungrateful."

"And you don't want him to stop."

"Because eventually maybe he'll get it right."

"Because *he* is right, and you're waiting for him to realize it."

Kinzi shook his head. "Look, I appreciate what you're doing..."

She leaned across the table. "I want to help you."

His eyes widened. The brief glimpse of hope was all she needed to see before he closed his expression again. "Do you have someone else to take care of you?"

"I take care of myself," she snapped. "I'm paraplegic, not helpless."

"Sorry," he said.

"And stop apologizing."

He snapped his muzzle shut, amused. "Why do you want to help?"

She looked into his dark brown eyes. "I met someone. Through the law school study groups. He came to visit once. I told Hay my girlfriends in class were taking me to dinner to celebrate graduation." She twisted her napkin in her paws, then dropped it on her empty plate. "I'm moving in a week and a half."

Kinzi raised his eyebrows. "And you haven't told him? Hasn't he noticed you packing?"

Carmila shook her head slowly. "I don't have much stuff. All my things from...from before are still in boxes. I have some clothes, some books. The apartment came furnished."

"I accumulate things." Kinzi waved a paw, with a bit of a smile. "In four years, I'd fill an entire room with just stuff."

"You have a life," she said. "I had Hayward, and law school."

"That's a bit dramatic," he said, but his smile faded. "Forgive me, but if that's all your life was, then isn't it a bit, well, shitty to pick up and move without even telling him, much less consulting with him?"

"It was a hard decision." The lie came more easily because she knew it should be true.

"And you couldn't talk..."

"I know!" She felt the pressure in her throat again. "I never intended to hurt him," she said, trying to calm down, reflecting that lawyers and lovers have a similar delicate precision with their language. "But it's not healthy for him to just keep going as if..." As if Foster's still around. "...as if we'll be roommates forever. It's not healthy for me."

The coyote drummed his fingers on the tabletop. "Nice that you're taking care of yourself."

Though his tone was neutral, she winced. "I'm a...I'm a bitch." No, you're not, Pinz would tell her, but it was okay if Kinzi thought she was. "But I kept putting off telling him, because I wasn't sure about Pinz. And then when I was, I knew it would hurt him, and..."

The hardness in his eyes was gone. She pressed her fingers to her own eyes. "I'm going to tell him tomorrow," she said. "So maybe you'd want to call tonight and see what he's doing tomorrow night. He might need someone to hang out with."

Kinzi rubbed his muzzle. "And it would make you feel better about abandoning him."

Carmila picked up her napkin again. She sighed, pulling it apart with her claws. "Not only that. I really want him to be happy."

The waiter walked up with their sandwiches. Kinzi looked at him, then back at Carmila. He shook his head. "I don't think so."

Her muzzle snapped up. "What?" The waiter looked between them, holding the plates, making no move to put them down.

Kinzi stood up, pulled out his wallet, and dropped two twenties on the table. "Lunch is on me, and dessert if you want it. I appreciate your thoughtfulness, but I'm otherwise occupied tomorrow night."

"But...wait!" She wheeled herself out from around the table to confront him. "But you want him."

He took off his glasses and rubbed his eyes. "Yes," he said, and replaced the glasses to look down at her. "But not like this. Not on the rebound from a fake relationship he constructed so he wouldn't have to get over losing his partner. If it's meant to be, he'll come to me in his own time."

A pair of fennecs at the next table looked over. The waiter put their sandwiches down and hesitated one more moment before walking quickly away. Carmila ignored them all. "Please. I really need your help."

Kinzi met her eyes, his ears splayed. "I know you told me not to apologize anymore," he said, his deep voice soft, "but I'm sorry."

He turned and walked quickly enough that she would have to hurry to catch him, his tail flat down his legs. She leaned one elbow on the table and watched him open the glass door, feeling empty again.

H

Carmila talked Hayward into a booth at Angelica's, even though they both liked the outdoor garden. She refused his help as she lifted herself onto the soft leather. "I'm tired of sitting in that chair," she said as the waiter came over to move the chair out of the way, behind the booth. Fleetingly, Carmila was glad he was a skunk; the chair smelled strongly like her, and on the rare occasions when a non-Hayward canid got close enough to smell, she usually saw his nose wrinkle.

Hayward smiled his chipper smile. "I know what you mean," he said. "Iced tea, please, and a Monte Cristo."

"Coke, and a tuna on whole wheat," she told the waiter, who nodded and left.

"No Monte Cristo for you?"

"Not today." She rubbed a finger over a greasy patch on the faux-wood tabletop.

"Nice to get a break from studying for the bar exam?" He grinned.

She watched the waiter prepare their drinks. She'd have to wait until he delivered them. "Nice to get a break from parties and sex?"

"Fox does not live by cock alone."

She loved his carefree acceptance of his own lifestyle. "It's hard to tell when you have time to fit anything else in that muzzle."

He raised an eyebrow. "Do you think about it that much?"

She rolled her eyes. "I try not to. But I see you eyeing the waiter."

He snapped his head back toward her. "He's straight, anyway." His smile broadened. "Glad I can be entertaining."

"Your main competition is legal briefs and practice exams." Until recently, she started to say, but he leaned his head to the side and spoke up first.

"Do you want some porn?"

The laugh burst out of her before she could stop it. "God, no. No, I'm good, thank you."

"I have some good short films," he said teasingly, just as the skunk came back. "Very artistic."

"Your sandwiches will be up in just a few minutes," the waiter said.

"Thanks." Hayward raised a paw as he left, following the waggle of his tail. "Pity. Anyway, I thought you liked the gay stuff. Are you into girls now?"

"No, I still like guys." She took a breath and then, before he could say anything, plunged on. "One particular guy, actually."

His ears perked up. "Really? That's great!" He reached across to take her paws, tail thumping against the seat. "I'm so happy for you! Tell me about him."

He was as happy as if he'd just found another boy to fuck. She resisted the initial instinct to pull her paws back. "His name's Pinz. He's an arctic fox, another law student. I met him through the study groups online. He was the only one smarter than me."

Hayward nodded, his eyes bright. "Where's he live?"

"Just north of Freestone."

He grinned. "Is he hung?"

She glared. "Hay." Then she remembered her promise to Pinz and said, "Like a bear. Actually."

"How many bears have you seen?"

"There are a lot of porn sites on the net," she said.

Hayward nodded. "No substitute for the real thing, though. Going to visit him?"

She took a drink of Coke and didn't meet his eyes. "I'm...going to live with him."

The whole restaurant seemed to go quiet. His grip on her paws didn't loosen, but the noise of his tail stopped. She heard his breathing, slow and even. God, say something, she pleaded silently. Finally, he did. "How long have you known him?"

"Six months."

His paws seemed locked around hers. "You never told me."

She shook her head. "I don't tell you about a lot of things." But the remark felt cruel, because his defenses were so clearly down. She softened her voice. "It was...at first it wasn't serious, and then it was, and I couldn't think how to. I..."

Guilt swallowed the rest of her words. She tried to fire up her anger at him for putting her in this situation, but the warm, delicate touch of his paws around hers pulled the anger out of her as easily as if it were nothing but a loose thread in the weave of her shirt.

"Don't be sorry," he said. "Things happen. You have your own life." He paused. "You'll have to take the bar exam there. I don't know how different it is."

"I am taking it there, Hay," she said. She met his eyes and felt the tension of the moment, which made her drop her muzzle. She stared at her plate. "Next week."

Then he released her paws.

She knew she'd eaten the sandwich, because her plate was empty, but there was no memory of it in her mind. She'd told Hay that Pinz wanted to meet him, that he'd be coming next Saturday morning to drive her back, and he'd promised to be there, expressing his happiness again in a horrible kind of forced cheer that made her want to cry. Somehow she managed, held herself together the way she had for years, with anger at the world, but it was ten times harder because it was her doing it this time, not some drunk beaver, and the people who'd put her in this position were herself and Hayward. "Come on," she told him in her most upbeat voice, aware that she sounded as forced as he did. "Don't pretend you won't be happy to have me out of your fur."

He nodded, silent. "Or you can get your own place," she went on. "One that's not handicapped-accessible. Counters you don't have to bend over to work on. Course, I don't know. Maybe you like that."

"I'll do something," he said.

"It's month-to-month. You can move out in July if you find a place."

"Yeah." He smiled. "I'm really happy for you. I can't wait to meet him."

But when they got home, he retreated to his bedroom, staying there for half an hour until he came out dressed in his loose silk shirt. "I've got a poetry reading," he said, "and a party later. But I'll be around tomorrow morning to help you pack."

"Is Kinzi going to be at the party?" she blurted out.

He tilted his muzzle, honest curiosity displacing his mask for a moment. "I don't think so. Why?"

"He called for you yesterday. He sounds nice. Better than most of the tail-chasers you waste your time with."

He smiled, the mask back in place. "Thanks, Carm, but I'll find him someone nice. I have a couple people in mind. One of them will be at the party."

"Who are they?" she called as he put his paw on the door.

He stopped, and then opened the door. "I'll tell you tonight," he said, and walked out.

Pinz was glad she'd told him. "He'll be okay," he said on the phone when she called him, wanting to hear his voice. "It's like breaking up. He'll get over it, I promise."

"I guess so." She bit her lip, knowing she shouldn't say what she was thinking, but knowing it would eat at her if she didn't. "Maybe I could just come out there to take the bar? Not move out there just yet?"

"You know, a verbal contract is binding in both our states." Pinz sounded more amused than anything else.

And she loved that about him, that he knew when she was serious but didn't want to be taken seriously. How had he gotten to know her so well over the phone, over chat rooms, with only the one brief weekend together in person? But she knew him too, well enough that she felt comfortable suggesting that they tear up all their carefully-laid plans, knowing he wouldn't let her. "I know," she said, and smiled into the phone, rubbing her eyes. "You're the one who has experience with breakups."

"I've never lost a brother," he said.

"I know, but—"

"I misplaced an aunt once, but we found her at the park an hour later."

She laughed, and cried a little bit too, because she could hide it in the laughter. "God, how many nights did I lie there and wait for him to come back and think he should just have his own life? We were so different that the only thing keeping us together was a ghost. But I miss him already."

Pinz was quiet. She went on, "I know I'll get over it and he will too."

He chuckled softly. "It's because it hurts that you know it's worthwhile. Right?"

Carmila rubbed her eyes again. Her fingers came away damp. "You're right. You're always right." He blew a kiss to her through the phone line. "Do you know how annoying that is?"

"I count on it, darling."

She waited up late that night for Hayward, studying as best she could, but when she dozed off in front of her computer, she knew she had to get to bed. He wasn't there in the morning when she woke up, either, which wasn't unusual; he often spent the night somewhere. But this time, she couldn't help but think he was avoiding her, or the apartment, or both. She took a bath, relaxing in the warm water, but even that wasn't enough to put her mind at ease.

The price of the bath was getting out of it, when her fur was soaked and heavy and the air was cold, but she had enough undercoat left to keep her warm. So she draped a towel over her chair, pulled herself into it, and wheeled herself over to the large living room window, where the summer sun warmed her and dried her fur.

And of course, because she was naked in the living room, Hayward picked that moment to come back. At least she knew he wouldn't be accompanied by anyone.

He smiled at her, lifting his nose in the air, but the smile was faded. "Took a bath?"

She sniffed back at him in return. "You should try it sometime."

He walked over to stand by the window, near her without looking, though he'd seen her naked many times. The first year, she'd needed his help to bathe or shower. "It's going to be weird without you."

"Imagine, you'll be able to bring people over here. You can have the lower bunk. You won't have to worry about the smell of other boys on the sheets."

"I don't worry about that," he said softly.

"You should," she said. "You boys stink after you've been going at it."

His breath clouded the glass. "Did you start packing already?"

"Don't worry about it," she said. "I don't have a whole lot."

"Clothes," he said. "Books. The computer. Boxes downstairs." He paused. "There's a box in the closet..."

"If I haven't touched it in four years, I don't need it."

His ears flattened. "You should have it," he said.

She looked at his profile, limned with sunlight, a crescent gleam off his eye. Slowly, she wheeled herself back to her room, where she pulled a shirt on and draped a blanket over her lap. Before she closed the closet door, she looked in the back corner, at the U-Haul box and the four-year-old tape sealing it shut. Memories fluttered at the edge of her mind. She shut the door and wheeled herself back out into the sunlight.

Hayward had started breakfast in the kitchen. She rolled to her desk and opened another practice exam. She smelled eggs cooking, and then onions, and knew he was making the onion and pepper omelette she liked, the one he was so good at. When he brought it out, she put her practice exam aside to join him at the coffee table. They ate in silence for a while, until Hayward said, "Can he cook?"

"He says he can. Maybe not as good as you."

"Most everyone can do an omelette." He took a drink of juice. "Shim once burned hard-boiled eggs."

She had to laugh. "I knew you'd know someone who can't cook eggs."

He shrugged. His smile was still a watered-down version of his usual one, and his tail was just hanging as limply as hers did. "I know a couple people who can't," he said.

She couldn't think of anything to say to that. But after he'd finished, when she'd insisted on washing up, he just nodded and went down to get some boxes he'd bought the other night. Before she'd finished the dishes, he'd already put together two boxes for her. "I can do that," she said, and he gave her that limp smile again.

"Christ," she exploded, "will you yell at me or something?"

Hayward winced slightly and flicked an ear. "I'm not angry."

"Why not? I give you one week's notice and you just give me that 'oh, okay' look and your tail looks like it's been left out in the rain." His tail perked up a little at that. "I'd be furious at me!"

"You didn't mean to hurt me," he murmured, looking down into one of the empty boxes. "You're right, it's about time you moved on."

"See?" She smacked the arm of her chair. "This is why I didn't tell you earlier. I didn't want to live with Hayward the Martyr for a month."

"Carm," he said, "all I ever wanted for you was happiness. If I knew any straight guys who deserved you, I'd have introduced you ages ago."

She bit her tongue. "Really? Because all I wanted for you was for you to get a damn clue and move on with your life."

"My life is fine," he said softly.

"Sure it is," she said, leaning back to look at him. "Sure it is."

He grinned down at her. "You really care."

"Pff." She waved a paw.

"It's not like I won't see you again."

"Oh, I'm sure you're going to come all the way out to Freestone."

He leaned down, his smile wider now. "There's gay guys out in Freestone. I'm sure I can entertain myself."

The light was coming in more strongly now, the sun angled to spread across the floor. The whole room glowed softly with reflected light, and Hayward's eyes gleamed to match. She flicked her ears and looked up at him. "What, you've gone through all the ones here?"

He shook his head. "Not even close. But I want to see what kind of life you make for yourself."

"Pinz has an uncle in a law firm. He says with the Orwell laws, I should be able to get something easily."

"Also because you're smart."

She waved that away. "I have good job prospects and a great guy. It's a lot to look forward to."

"He'd be so proud of you."

She didn't have to ask who he meant. "I know."

He smiled. "I'll help you start packing," he said, brushed her ear with his muzzle and walked into the bedroom.

She hugged her arms around herself, staring down at the box. Her fur prickled with premonitory dread, and when he came out with the small box, the tape peeling from its top, she lowered her ears.

"You can keep that," she said.

"No, it's okay." He smiled as though he were bestowing a blessing. "I want you to have it."

"Hay, just keep it."

He shook his head. His smile wavered only slightly. "I have other pictures and stuff."

She steeled herself. "I don't want it," she said.

It would have been cowardly not to watch the hurt in his eyes, the loss of his smile, his large black ears sagging, dropping. It had been bad yesterday, but he'd gotten over it. Today it was worse, because it was that much closer to the sharp truth at the center that she was trying not to cut him with. He was bleeding anyway, if not as badly as he could be. But it was close enough. "Carm..." he began, and then stopped, looking down at the box.

"I don't want it," she said again. "You should throw it out."

His fingers clenched around the box. "I really think you'll want it."

"Keep it, then," she said. "It's your...decision." She'd been a hair from saying "funeral."

"If you ever want it, just—"

"I don't want it!" She couldn't keep her voice down, her stomach churning, her head hot as if she had a fever. "I don't want it, Hay, and I never will!"

"Listen," Hayward said, his voice tighter than she'd ever heard it, "don't...don't throw away..."

"It's been four years," she snapped. "You told me it's time to move on."

She hadn't seen him cry since the week after the funeral, but he looked like he was about to. He turned and walked stiffly back, his tail wrapped tightly around his left leg.

She almost said the rest of it then, because things were already so bad that telling him could hardly make it worse. Before she could work herself up to it, he turned around. "All we want is for you to be happy."

"We?" She stared. "Who's 'we'?"

The box slipped; he reseated it in his arms. "I want you to be happy," he said. "Foster would have, too."

He disappeared into the bedroom. She stared down at the open, empty box. She knew he talked to Foster sometimes, but now she was actually a little bit worried about him. When he didn't come back out, she wheeled herself in after him.

He was sitting on her bunk, a stack of her clothes beside him, staring at the wall. When he heard her, he stood up quickly. "Here," he said, picking up the stack and holding them out. "I'll get another pile ready."

"Thanks." She took them, started to say something, then stopped when he turned his back on her and walked to her dresser.

It took them only that afternoon to pack her boxes, and they did it in near-total silence. Ten boxes of varying sizes sat in the living room when they were done: her clothes, her books, one box of odds and ends, one open box for toiletries and other last-minute things. Hayward put the open box on the ground where she could reach it, and then said, "I've got a dinner to go to. Um, with Kinzi and..." He waved a paw. "Boris."

He needed the time alone, so she didn't call him on the lie. She didn't want to be with him anyway, not this quiet, moping Hayward. But the apartment was hardly more cheerful without him. The monument of boxes reminded her every time she looked at them how little there was to her life. Even when she stared resolutely at her computer screen, away from the neatly-stacked pile, the smell of new cardboard reached her. The carnations didn't cover it, so she had to open the window even though the day was chilly.

The fresh air perked her ears up, and Pinz was on the computer to console her. She didn't tell him her worry about Hayward, only that she'd told him and it hadn't gone as well as she'd have liked. He said all the right things, ending with the rightest thing of all:

PinzColler: I'll be there in a week.

She hugged herself again and imagined his fingers on her arms.

She barely saw Hayward for the next week, but at least he didn't make any more worrying references to Foster when she did see him. Stress, she told herself. One night, she stayed up as late as she could, just to see when he came back. When he finally did, she was half-asleep at her desk, and the next morning, she barely remembered their conversation. If he hadn't left clothes draped all over the floor and the furniture, she would have thought he'd spent most of the week at friends' houses.

The clothes stayed where they were until Saturday morning, when she wheeled herself around the apartment picking them up in a frenzy. Pinz was due at ten, and as much as she would have liked to have left the apartment sloppy and messy, to show him what she was leaving, the impulse to clean overwhelmed her Saturday morning when she let the morning light in onto piles of discarded vests and jeans and silk shirts. She gathered them all up and threw them into the bathroom hamper, and then attacked the kitchen with a sponge.

Hayward was still asleep, or pretending; she could smell him. He didn't stir through her alarm and her cleaning, nor when the doorbell rang, nor even when the door opened and Pinz said, in the deep voice she'd grown to love, "I've come to Gateway to find the loveliest fox here and take her home, and this is my hundredth stop, so—ah, it looks like my search is over."

She beamed up. He closed the door and dropped to one knee. His short-sleeved blue print shirt fell open to show his fluffy chest ruff. "Hi, darling," she said.

He took her paw. "You've grown more beautiful in the last two months. You probably didn't notice." He lifted her paw and kissed it gently.

"Silly," she said. "You're a lawyer through and through. Buttering up the witness."

"As long as you're a friendly witness."

She reached out and hugged him, and he felt warm and alive against her. "So," he said, eyeing the pile of boxes, "this is it, huh? Looks smaller than in the picture."

"Do you have enough room?"

"I've made plenty." He looked around the apartment, lifted his nose. The sun caught his short ears, the gentle slope of his forehead, his short, round muzzle. "The place smells great. Oh, you haven't thrown out the flowers yet."

The carnations were brown and wilted. They smelled old, but Carmila hadn't been able to bring herself to get rid of them. Apparently she'd gotten so accustomed to the delicate smell of decay that she hadn't noticed. "I—"

"I got you new ones." He smiled, getting to his feet. "They're at my place, though. Or they will be, when we get there tomorrow. So, um," he looked around the apartment.

"Asleep," she said.

"Ah." His ears fell, just a little. "Well, let's move this to the car, shall we?"

He'd brought a van with the rental company's name splashed on the side. Her boxes took up just over half of it. She watched him stack the last one in place and thought, that's my life in there. He turned to smile at her and said, "One last look around the apartment? See if there's anything you forgot?"

She'd gone through it twice on Friday. "Sure," she said.

They looked in on the kitchen and the bathroom, where her ears flushed and flattened at the pile of clothes, the thicker smell of Hayward's stronger musk. But Pinz just said, "He smells like a nice guy."

As they walked back past the open bedroom door, Hayward's voice said, "You must be Pinzer."

He was standing beside his bed, dressed only in a pair of his old black boxers, the hems frayed. His fur stuck out every which way, and his scent was even stronger than it had been in the bathroom. Through half-lidded eyes, he was watching Pinz, not even looking at her. That hurt, but she told herself coldly that she deserved it.

"Mister Hayward, I presume." Pinz walked in and stuck out a paw as casually as if they were both at a party.

"Pleasure to meet you," Hayward said. He shook paws, then coughed into his own. "Sorry about..." He waved down at himself.

"Sorry to disturb you. I understand you keep late hours."

"Yeah, I..." Hayward scratched behind his ears. Carmila had never seen him this ill at ease, never. He glanced over his shoulder, up at his bed. At the picture she'd never seen. But he didn't say anything, so she didn't, either.

"Well," Pinzer said, with a look down at Carmila, "we need to get on the road. Long trip ahead."

Hayward nodded. "Take care of her," he said.

"I can take care of myself," she snapped.

He looked at her, then. His golden eyes blinked once. She waited for him to walk forward to hug her, until it occurred to her that he was waiting for her to come to him. She rolled in, slowly, and reached around his waist. He leaned over, putting an arm around her shoulders and brushing her ear with his muzzle. "So long, Carm," he said softly.

"Good-bye," she said. His pain was all the more unbearable because she felt it only in sympathy, as she sometimes dreamed she could feel her feet tingling. He and Pinz, they both expected her to feel the same wrenching at leaving him that he was feeling, when all she felt was an overwhelming sadness for him. She had to wheel herself out of the stuffy air there, quickly, before her secret escaped her.

The living room now looked almost the same as it had for four years, with her boxes gone and the carnations in the garbage. Only her computer was missing from the desk. It looked as lifeless as a painting, still and quiet with the windows closed. It was no wonder Hayward talked to Foster, she thought. The wonder was that she hadn't.

She half-expected Hayward to follow Pinz out, but the only thing she heard was the creak of him climbing back into bed. Pinz looked a little worried, and took one glance back before saying, "We could wait a bit." She met his eyes. He thought her emotion was about leaving Hayward. "If you want."

"No," she whispered, and in this way she was able to tell him her terrible secret, the thing she couldn't tell Hayward, and he would never know how much it hurt her to cut the bonds, how much she needed to be free. But he didn't have to understand. All he had to do was hear the words. "I want to go." And then the words were out and gone, and Pinz smiled and nuzzled her ears, and he didn't hate her, and her heart felt lighter.

The sun warmed her fur, out in the street. The door to her building closed behind her with a final, hollow thunk. At the van, she looked back, though she knew she wouldn't see Hay. "He'll be okay," she said.

Pinz smiled and clasped her shoulder. "I'm sure he will," he said. He lifted her into the seat and stowed her chair in the back.

She loved the way he agreed with her. It almost convinced her that she was right.

CHAPTER 5: JULY

Kinzi panted, coming out of the summer heat into the air-conditioned travel agency. He buttoned up his loose cotton shirt as he padded up to the reception desk. The small clock on the desk in the grove of plastic palm trees, flanked by grass-skirted dancing otters, read 4:25.

"Can I help you, sir?" the receptionist, a ringtail, said in a bright, professional voice.

The tall coyote smiled back, leaning on the desk. "I'm here for Hayward." He nodded toward the back, where the red fox was looking at him with some surprise, a headset attached to his large black ear.

The ringtail's professional smile became a smirk. "Go right on back," he said.

Hayward's conversation became clearer to Kinzi's focused ears as he walked back. "You don't want to visit the desert?" His ears lowered. "Okay. Let me transfer you. Hold, please." He hit a button on his phone and leaned back in his chair with a sigh. "Mella, line three."

The squirrel next to him picked up the line and started talking, bright and animated. Hayward closed his eyes for a moment, and then looked up at Kinzi, a wan smile back in place. "Hi there."

"Long time," Kinzi said.

"Only a month." Hayward looked him up and down. "You look good."

"So do you," Kinzi said automatically, though it was a lie. Hayward's eyes were drooping, his ears hadn't even come all the way back up, and though he was wearing a nice silk shirt, it was draped over mussed fur, not the soft, clean ruff Kinzi remembered.

"What brings you here?"

Kinzi pointed. "You, swishy."

Hayward's tail wagged gently. "I know that, but why today?"

"Oh, you haven't been around much. I thought I'd come see how you've been. Want to grab a drink?"

"Sure." The red fox glanced at the clock and got up from his desk.

At the back of the room, a badger cleared his throat. "Actually, Hay, if you could stick around 'til closing time and meet your quota, that'd be great."

The marten who sat across from Hayward snickered. Hayward looked at Kinzi, and then sat down resignedly.

Kinzi rubbed his chin, feeling out of place in the busy office floor. He motioned to the front as Hayward picked up the phone again, and the fox nodded to him.

The ringtail ignored him as he leaned on the desk, staring thoughtfully back at Hayward. What *was* he doing here? He'd hit his fortieth birthday not too long ago, when everything appeared to be going great, and then Jake had left him and his friend Boris had set him up with Hayward, and things had gone on from there.

He was too old to bounce between twenty-something dates forever, he knew. The mirror reminded him every day. So why not just thank Hayward and start hanging out in coffee shops, or hobby clubs, or wherever else you could find old queers whose ex-boyfriends preferred younger meat?

There was something about Hayward, though, not to steal a movie title. His quiet assurance, his joy in other people's happiness, the mystery surrounding his own life. Kinzi had guessed that there was some person in Hayward's background even before he'd talked to Carmila. Since talking to her, he'd been torn between intruding on Hayward's privacy and wanting desperately to help. When Hayward felt better, when he was over his sister's leaving, Kinzi'd start going on dates again, and he'd push things forward slowly, he'd decided. Maybe suggest a single date instead of a double, once.

Last night, though, he'd gotten a phone call that had convinced him he couldn't wait that long. And seeing Hayward now, dull and unkempt, he knew the fox needed him. That thought filled him with nervous energy, tapping a claw on the counter until the receptionist glared at him; it also filled him with worries, because what if he couldn't help? What if he wasn't what Hayward needed? Or, worse, what if he was, but it was too much of a burden?

At five to five, Hayward's boss said something, and Hayward nodded and stood, arranging the papers on his desk. He tapped a code into his phone and waved good-byes to the others, who were doing the same.

As he passed the desk, the ringtail said, "Have a niiiice time." Hayward ignored him and held the door for Kinzi, who braced himself for the heat and stepped outside.

They didn't talk until they were two blocks from Hay's office, when Kinzi broke the silence. "You haven't called me for a date in a while."

They'd turned onto a street that was caught between cute and seedy, with a few trendy coffee shops that sat mostly empty, some vacant storefronts that had once been gift and jewelry stores, and two restaurants that still seemed to be doing well. At the end of the street and a block to the right was a nice bar, which was where Kinzi was headed.

"Sorry." Hayward reached up to rub a paw through his head fur, leaving it more ruffled. "Summer. Lots of people are away, and I've been kind of busy."

"Oh? What's been keeping you busy?"

Hayward looked down at the soft grass they were walking on. They passed a few outdoor tables, the scents of tomato sauce and garlic, and soft accordion music. It wasn't until they stopped at the next light that he said, "You know, seeing people. Trying to find someone for Jock."

"The cougar? The one who liked 'Meet The Pattersons'? The one who said 'Police School 2' was better than 'Cab Driver' because 'Cab Driver' was, quote, not funny, unquote?"

Hayward raised his eyebrows. Ahead of them, a pair of rabbits crossed the street, holding paws. "There's someone out there for everyone."

Kinzi looked ahead to the bar and said, "What about you?"

"I've got someone." The familiar response was automatic, said without feeling, but more insistently than in the past.

"I'd like to meet him sometime."

Kinzi'd said that before, too, before he'd known who Hayward was talking about, and Hayward had always changed the subject. Now the fox smiled and said, "We're going to the Three Corners, aren't we?"

The bar was just a half-block ahead of them. They'd met there twice before. "It'll be happy hour in, let's see, twenty minutes." Kinzi checked his phone. "Why don't you call your someone, have him meet us there?"

"I can wait," Hayward said, apparently in response to the upcoming happy hour.

"Swishy," Kinzi said. Hayward's ears flicked. "I'm worried about you."

Hayward kept walking, to the door of the bar. He flashed a smile up at the coyote as he held the door open for him. "You don't have to worry about me."

There weren't many people in the bar, a bright place with four TVs and Tiffany ceiling lights. They sat at an isolated corner of the bar, behind the beer taps. The bartender, a tall otter in a gold vest, came over. "You boys gonna wait 'til happy hour?" she said.

Kinzi nodded, and she put a bowl of pretzels out. "Thanks," the coyote said, reaching for one. Hayward just looked at the bowl. In the bright, cheery bar, he looked even more out of place.

"Seriously, though," Kinzi said. "You look like shit, you know that, right? Cause if you don't, I might have to take away your gay license."

"It's just been a rough couple days." Hayward brought his paw up to smooth his head fur. It helped a little.

"Just a couple days? You haven't returned any of my messages for a month." Hayward opened his mouth, but Kinzi cut him off. "Listen, Hay, I've known you for almost a year now. I know there's people known you a lot longer than that, but none of the friends of yours I know seem all that worried. 'Hay just does his own thing,' Boris said, 'he'll come back around soon.' I dunno, but that doesn't really work with me."

Hayward shrugged. "They're right," he said, but his tail arched up a little.

Kinzi tapped a finger on the bar. "How many of them know that your sister moved to Freestone a month ago?"

The red fox's muzzle jerked toward Kinzi, his eyes widening. The way his mouth parted as he searched for something to say was so adorable it made Kinzi smile, despite the subject matter. "I...my sister? I told you...I don't have..."

Hayward was staring at him, more off-balance than the coyote'd ever seen him. "I called your machine a couple months ago. She picked up and talked to me. She was worried about how you'd react when she left."

"Oh." Hayward's ears stayed perked, but his expression relaxed. "She's doing well. Pinzer's a great guy. Really cute, smart, and he's head over heels for her."

"Glad she found someone," Kinzi said. "She sounded really happy."

If Hayward caught the emphasis on the first "she," he didn't let on. "So what did she tell you?"

No need to tell him he knew about Foster. Not yet. "Just that she'd met someone and was leaving, and she was worried you'd take it badly. Can't imagine why she thought that."

Hayward tapped the bar. "And today? Did she call you again to ask you to check up on me?"

"No," Kinzi lied. "I remembered talking to her and wondered if you were still moping." He checked the clock again. Five twenty-five.

"I'm not moping." Hayward said sharply. "Just...everyone's paired up now, and the ones that aren't don't want to be."

"Like Jock?"

The fox snorted. "He called and asked if I knew anyone who gave good blow jobs and free samples."

Kinzi shook his head. "He really liked talking to you about his high school sports. Now you've got a friend for life."

"He's not a bad guy, just young. I thought a good older guy, more experienced, could be good for him." He looked up at the coyote. "And he'd bring a lot of life and energy to a relationship."

"I had that with Jake. Too much energy."

Hayward's ears lowered. "We went out on a date with Chet. He was quiet."

"I could never do that thing you did with him." He waved away the fox's raised eyebrow. "Not *that*. I mean, where you asked him just the right question. After you left, we sat there for fifteen minutes and I asked him like five things and he said two words."

The fox's ears came up. He straightened on the stool. "You could do it if you wanted," he said. "What about Mikka?"

"He never figured out you're not really interested in cars." Kinzi didn't stop to let the fox, now looking intently at him, respond. "I guess I'm looking for someone a little more mature. Someone who can still go out and have fun, but who doesn't mind having a quiet drink alone, who appreciates family and friends." Kinzi signaled the bartender and pointed at the 'Forest Night' tap in front of them.

"Like Opie?" Hayward rubbed his muzzle.

Kinzi vaguely recalled the ferret, one of the first Hayward had set him up with. That date had been the first time Kinzi'd taken the fox under the tail, and he still remembered the first time he'd felt that tight warmth, the length of Hayward in his paw, the muscular body shuddering below him. Hayward's whispered request to use Kinzi's place, taking the coyote into his confidence, stayed with him far more than anything the ferret had talked about at dinner. "He squeaks a lot when he comes."

The bartender, setting down their beers, gave Kinzi a raised eyebrow. "Boys," she said, shaking her head.

Hayward waited 'til she'd gone to tend to another customer. "That was it? That's why you never called him?"

Kinzi shrugged. "There wasn't a spark. I didn't sit around after and think, hey, I should call him again."

"You got along pretty well at dinner. You're both from around here. And he liked that movie, what was it, the war one?"

"A Bridge Too Far," Kinzi nodded. "He had good taste. I mean...well, you'd know better than I would."

"I set him up with Devon. They're still dating."

"As of a month ago."

Hayward's ears drooped. "Yes."

"Did anyone else take you as long as I have?"

"Fin. A swift fox." Hayward lapped at his beer. "I knew him for a year and a half. He's seeing an adorable fennec now. *They're* still doing okay. Fin would've called me otherwise."

"Everybody's probably fine." Kinzi took a long drink. "Almost everybody."

Hayward let out a long sigh. "What do you want?" he said. "You want me to admit it's been difficult?"

"That'd be a start."

"Fine." His ears were all the way down. He reached up and scratched the fur between them, leaving it mussed. "It's been difficult. I'll get through it."

"Hay," Kinzi started, but the fox raised a paw and then stood, his beer still half-full.

"I really appreciate this hon," he said. "But I just need some time on my own."

Even then, Hay stood patiently waiting for Kinzi to accept his leaving. To be honest, Kinzi was pretty close. Who wanted a guy who shut himself off from the world, who wouldn't take any help, who preferred to be mired in his own depression? He was a great guy, for sure, and in the good times he'd been everything Kinzi could want, but would the bad times always be this hopeless quagmire? How long would they go on?

Hayward was still looking at him with those golden eyes, and though he was smiling, the eyes were sad. Maybe it was just that he didn't know he had the option not to be alone. Maybe he didn't want to impose his troubles on Kinzi. That kind of consideration, Kinzi could appreciate, and it fit with the Hayward he'd come to know and love over the past several months, the guy who always knew the right thing to say, who never seemed tempted to snipe at someone or speak poorly of them, who managed to shield his own troubles off from everyone he knew with disarmingly graceful ease.

Kinzi saw the tired courtesy in the slight incline of Hayward's head. Affection bloomed in his chest, making his decision easy. "You don't have to be on your own," he said, holding the fox's eyes with his.

Hayward straightened, his smile fixed in place. "I have someone," he said again, with a touch of belligerence, as though daring the coyote to disagree.

"I know," Kinzi said, and forged ahead. "But you could have someone alive."

Hayward flinched. Kinzi bit back his apology, and just watched the pain in the fox's eyes flare up and subside, leaving them duller. "I'm..."

"Fine?" Kinzi finished for him, not wanting to hear the tired denial again. "I know 'fine.' I've fucked 'fine.'"

Behind him, he heard the clink of a glass and the otter's "tchah." He ignored her. Hayward tilted his muzzle, his eyes sad. "Is *that* what you want?"

"Swishy..."

"Cause you should've just said. *That's* no problem."

"I don't want to fuck you." Kinzi reached out, letting his paw fall back to his side when Hayward drew back. "I want to...I want to help you. I want to talk to you. Just me and you."

"I can't."

"You mean you won't."

"No, I can't. I can't do that to..." Hayward stopped, and lowered his eyes.

"Listen," Kinzi said, "You can't be faithful your whole life. He left you." Hayward started to protest. The coyote held a paw up. "It wasn't his fault. But he left you. How long's it been since you talked to anyone about it?"

Slowly, Hayward shook his head. Kinzi blinked. "Not even Carmila?"

"What would be the point of talking? Why dwell on it?"

"But you are dwelling on it." Kinzi stayed seated so Hayward could look at him at eye level.

"That's not...I didn't mean..."

Kinzi wanted to grab him and hug him right there. "Look, you want to make someone else happy, do this for me. Let me take you back to my place tonight. We'll grab takeout on the way, and we'll just sit and talk."

Hayward's eyes slid past Kinzi's shoulder, considering. "No," he said, finally.

Now, Kinzi reached out again, grasping Hayward's paw before the fox could pull back. "I know you don't want to drag me into it. I know you think it'll make me miserable. I know you think you're doing me a favor by keeping me out of it." Hayward's eyes widened, and his whiskers twitched; his expression lost some of its guardedness. "I understand what I'm getting into. I've known you for nine months. I want to know you better."

The struggle behind Hayward's eyes was plain enough even if the fox weren't biting his lip. Eyes dropped to Kinzi's chest, he said, "No."

"Hay—"

The fox took a breath. "If you're going to do this, then we might as well do it all the way."

Kinzi raised his eyebrows. Hayward's smile was tentative, but brighter than any Kinzi'd seen on him yet that day. "I mean...if we go to your place, it'll be too easy. Nobody's been in my place but me and Carm... and Pinzer...for years." Kinzi tried not to let his eyes widen too much. Hayward's smile faded. "Unless you don't want to."

"I want to." Kinzi stood. "Very much."

They picked up Chinese food, chicken lo mein and orange chicken, and Hayward suggested the steamed pork buns as well. It didn't surprise Kinzi when the shy red panda who brought their order out perked up and smiled when he saw Hayward, and put the food down to hug him. While they exchanged a few words, he watched, and asked himself, is this okay? It's going to be like this all over Gateway, people recognizing him, and you'll know there's about a ninety percent chance that they had their dick in him somewhere, sometime. Will that bother you?

It did, but only a little, and it was a bothering like the heartburn from the spicy ribs at his favorite barbecue place: the price of admission for a unique and wonderful experience. He knew Hay didn't form attachments, so the fact that he'd sucked off (probably) the red panda didn't mean anything, really.

"He and Ku aren't together anymore, but he met another panda and he's happy. What's funny?"

Kinzi chuckled. "I was just thinking that whenever we meet someone like that, I'm going to be guessing whether he was in your muzzle or under your tail."

Hayward started to say something and then flicked his ears before speaking. "And what was your guess with Wing?"

"Muzzle."

Hayward raised an eyebrow. "He was a tail, actually. You think he's shy, you should've seen Ku."

"I wouldn't have guessed." Kinzi swung the bag of food at his side.

"Clearly." Hayward rubbed his muzzle. "How many guys have you been with?"

"Ever?" Hayward nodded. Kinzi stared down at his paws, adding up in his head. "Not counting the ones I was with when I was with you, um, there was Jake, and then maybe four or five before him."

"But you weren't really with any of the ones with me."

"Oh, sure I was." Kinzi smiled. "I was with them through you. You're like..." He grasped for a metaphor.

Hayward brought his two paws together and then slowly pulled them apart, as if drawing out a piece of string. "A bridge. Between people on opposite river banks."

"Swishiest bridge I ever saw." Kinzi was glad to see Hayward's smile. "Y'always done this bridge thing, or just since, uh..."

"Just the last four years and ten months," Hayward said.

Kinzi filed away that information, pausing briefly to show he recognized the importance of it, then going on so as not to dwell on it. "I've never met anyone like you."

"We're all unique," Hayward said.

"Yes and no. Guys like Jock are a dime a dozen."

"Maybe," Hayward countered, "but how many of them are cougars who like salsa music? How many are completely opposite in taste in movies from you? How many of them eat their fries with mustard or pico instead of ketchup? Put all those together, and soon you come up with something that doesn't exist anywhere else."

"If you're going to take it to extremes," Kinzi said.

"It's not about extremes," Hayward said, his ears perked and tone stronger now. "It's about the little things. Everyone has little puzzle pieces that match, and fitting them together so that they stay is really wonderful."

"And you think there's only one set of puzzle pieces that matches each person?"

Hayward paused at the door of his apartment building, holding the key just in front of the waist-high lock. Then he slid it in and turned it, and opened the door without saying anything. He led Kinzi down the hall to a wide apartment door, unlocked it, and gestured him in.

Kinzi walked into a moderately spacious living room, in which all the furniture was lower to the ground than he was used to. He looked around the tasteful grey carpeting, the arctic icescapes on the walls, the wooden desk sitting bare beneath one of the windows, and the clothes strewn across the floor. "Sorry about the mess." Hayward went about collecting the clothes.

"No problem. Where are the plates?"

"Over the sink to the right," Hayward called as Kinzi set the food on the low counter and opened the cupboard. A picture on the shelf caught his eye: an arctic fox with bright blue eyes. He wore a loose blue shirt that matched his eyes, black shorts, and a wide, welcoming smile. Kinzi's first reaction had been the guilty start of an intruder, but it was impossible to hold onto that feeling in the light of the fox's smile. The coyote held the plates until he realized he was just staring at the photo.

By the time Hayward poked his head into the kitchen, Kinzi had prepared both plates. "Forks?" Hayward pointed to a drawer. Kinzi grabbed two forks from it and brought the plates out to the glass coffee table in the living room.

They sat on the small loveseat together facing the dark TV and ate, only breaking the silence to comment on how good the food was. Hayward took the empty plates when they were done and then came back to sit next to Kinzi, his tail falling between them.

"You don't want to watch anything?" Kinzi said.

Hayward shook his head. He leaned back into the corner of the loveseat and turned to face the coyote. "Nothing good on. I haven't turned this TV on in months, actually."

"Huh." Kinzi rested his paw on the fox's tail. It twitched under his fingers but didn't pull back. Was Hayward hoping things would get more physical? If he hadn't been with anyone, anyone at all, for a month... Kinzi knew he was getting tired of his own paw, lately. He could only imagine how Hay felt. "What have you been doing for the last month? I mean, really?"

Hayward's eyes went a bit distant. "Working. Eating out. Working out." He flicked his ears, and his voice became lower. "Playing around online. I'm not used to being alone."

"You and Carmila were that close?"

The fox straightened and sighed. "We lived together for four years."

But his voice was stronger, and Kinzi felt like he'd taken a wrong turn. "What about the other thing?" Hayward picked at the fur on his wrist. "I mean, that happened, what, four years ago? Five years ago?"

Hayward said, "It's complicated," and he looked like he was going to say more, but Kinzi leaned in and cut him off.

"Complicated? You lost someone. It sucks, I know."

Hayward's ears folded back, and his eyes flashed. "I didn't just lose *someone*. I lost the only guy I've ever loved." The low, raw tone was back in his voice, an edge that could mean he was close to either shouting or crying.

"You lost the only guy you ever let yourself love."

Hayward shook his head. "It was one of a kind."

Kinzi kept his voice level. "Don't you think he'd want you to be happy?"

"He wants me to help other people be happy!" Hayward raised his voice, then stopped. When he went on, his voice was calmer. "Wanted me to."

Kinzi's ears flicked down and back up. He decided to ignore the present tense. Hay was stressed, and if the worst thing he'd done this past month was talk to the ghost of his dead boyfriend, that wasn't so bad. "The thing about bridges," he said, "is people walk all over them. They don't give a shit about them until they fall down." He leaned closer, his nose an inch from Hayward's. "I don't want you to fall down."

Hay just stared back at him, his mouth slightly parted. Ah, the hell with it, Kinzi thought, and pressed his muzzle to the fox's, tongue pushing between those parted lips.

Hayward tensed. Slowly, his tongue curled against Kinzi's thicker one, and his body settled into the embrace. When his paw reached up to settle on Kinzi's hip, the coyote allowed himself to relax. He hadn't been sure how Hay would react; he'd never seen him full-muzzle kiss anyone. He hadn't been sure how he'd react, for that matter; he hadn't kissed anyone since Jake. But Hay was nothing like Jake. He was warm, earnest, and he was making a contented noise in the back of his throat. What's more, he and Kinzi were both getting warm in certain spots that were right next to each other as their bodies pressed together.

The coyote pushed his paws behind Hay's torso, pulling the muscular fox up against him, not letting his muzzle go. When Hay's arms tightened around him, and the fox's paw slipped down over his rear, he felt the momentum driving them to the bedroom, and as much as Kinzi wanted that, he needed to say certain things first. He disengaged from the kiss as gently as he could, his tongue lolling as he pulled his head back. "I've missed you," he said.

Hayward kept his paws linked just above Kinzi's tail. "Missed you too," he said softly.

"But...look, I hate to do this, but I'm not gonna drop this whole thing about taking care of you just because things get hot between us."

Confusion flickered through Hayward's ears momentarily, then cleared. "This isn't going to get resolved overnight," he said. "But I promise you, you can stay tonight, all night. We can talk more, if you want." His paw squeezed beneath Kinzi's tail. "After. And we can go out again tomorrow."

The warmth in Kinzi's sheath suffused his whole body. "Just tomorrow?" he said, claws teasing at the buttons on Hayward's shirt, casually undoing them.

Hayward glanced down at the paw. "Maybe more. We'll have to see how it goes," he said. When Kinzi hesitated, he leaned his nose forward to nuzzle at Kinzi's paw. "It might take me a little while to get used to this."

"You'd better," Kinzi said fiercely. "Because I have no intention of stopping."

The fox's muzzle came up to nuzzle under Kinzi's chin. "Good," he said, and then they were kissing again, tongues sliding past each other with warm, growing passion. Kinzi's paw, trapped between them, kept working at Hayward's shirt buttons, sliding inside to push fingers through his chest ruff. He'd pushed his fingers through the fox's fur many times, but this time, the unkempt fur made his caress feel more intimate, as though he were reaching through the veneer to the real Hayward. It was just the two of them on the small loveseat, his body pushing the smaller fox down into the cushions.

Hayward's paws kept busy as well, tugging Kinzi's shirt out of his pants and slipping under it to circle his sides, a less familiar sensation, but the fox's fingers knew just where to go, catching the line of Kinzi's hips even through the extra padding the coyote couldn't seem to get rid of. A little more kissing, and the paws pushed back, along the coyote's fur, below his tail to his rear.

"Mmm," Kinzi said, pulling his head up. "Not fair. I can't get my paw to your butt."

Hayward seemed to work himself further down into the couch. "You'll get plenty later." He gave Kinzi's rear another squeeze.

"Maybe I want this instead." Kinzi took his free paw and forced it between them, cupping the fox's hard shaft through his pants.

Hayward closed his eyes and parted his lips. "Oh, well," he breathed, "if you insist."

At which Kinzi lowered his muzzle and kissed the fox again, pushing into the long muzzle with his tongue, tasting passion and orange chicken, and mostly fox, a musky scent working its way through him until his tail tingled with it. Between his fingers, Hayward's shaft felt as solid as his own was, a warm, hard ridge he rubbed and pressed into while the fox's paws came around to undo the fasteners on his pants. He squirmed a little, but Hayward only took advantage of the loosened waist to push his paws further in, down the back of Kinzi's thighs and up along his rear again.

He'd opened three buttons on Hayward's shirt by that time, his paw finding the fox's ribcage and tight stomach. They passed an enjoyable several minutes kissing and nuzzling at each other's muzzles, stroking and groping, and Kinzi was surprised and pleased to find that when he pulled back again, there was a little sparkle in Hayward's eyes. Submerging in physical pleasure had a funny way of putting emotional issues on hold, but Kinzi knew better than to expect things to be completely resolved. How many bouts of make-up sex had he had with Jake? How many issues had that solved?

What he could expect was that they could both enjoy the moment and the few moments immediately to come, without the weight of loneliness hanging over them. When he rocked back to kneel on the cushions, Hayward got up and took his paw, leading him back to the bedroom without another word.

They made short work of their clothes, with no shyness or hesitation, their white stomachs and groins glowing softly in the late evening light. Hayward pulled the naked coyote to the lower of the two bunks in the room, then reached up to a shelf beside the top bunk for a small bottle. He flicked the top open, squirted liquid into his paw, and reached back under his own tail. Kinzi grasped his wrist gently.

"Put it here," he said, bringing the paw back to the fox's front and his thick, now fully-erect shaft. Kinzi closed Hayward's slick paw around it and guided it up and down, smiling at the fox's gasp and half-closed eyes.

"Now give me some." Kinzi held his paw out.

Hayward looked at him, panting slightly, ears askew. "I still need to..." He trailed off at Kinzi's firm headshake. "I don't?"

Kinzi took a pawful of the cool liquid. He reached back under his own tail, rubbing it in there as Hayward's eyes widened. "I've taken you plenty of times," he said. "You get to take me this time."

Hayward looked down to where his paw was still holding his cock, as if weighing it. "Um..."

"You don't want to?"

"It's just, I'm kinda big." His ears lowered.

Kinzi reached over and wrapped a paw around the large shaft, giving it a good, firm stroke. He brought his muzzle right up to Hayward's. "Don't apologize for what you are."

The fox's muzzle opened further to pant, the corners of his mouth stretching back. "You're just full of good advice tonight."

"Glad you think it's good." Kinzi kept stroking, because he enjoyed the sensation, and also because Hayward's paw had moved over to his shaft to return the favor. The fox's fingers, slender and warm, felt delightful on his tight hard skin, and he could feel his knot growing in response. At the base of Hayward's shaft, his knot was similarly swollen.

Hayward chuckled softly, a breathy panting chuckle with a soft whine behind it. "It's...a little too good...if you want me to finish anywhere but all over your paw."

By this time, the fox's knot looked seriously big, like, the size of a tennis ball. Kinzi felt a flicker of weakness in his resolve. But he coated it liberally with lube, turned, and lay on his back on the bed, pulling Hayward down between his knees. He wanted to do this once, for Hay, and though he might've wanted to have a little more alcohol in him, there wouldn't be a better night than tonight, no better time than now.

If the sheets on the bed held any scent other than aroused fox and coyote, Kinzi couldn't smell it. His pulse was racing already, throbbing in his shaft with Hayward's touch and the anticipation of more. When he looked up into Hayward's golden eyes, he saw the same excitement building there. Kinzi smiled, fancying he could feel Hayward's heartbeat matching his, pulse for pulse.

Hayward started with a slick finger pushed gently into the coyote, then another. Kinzi moaned softly, closing his eyes, relaxing at the rubbing touch. The fox's fingers stretched him gently, and when he added a third finger, it was only slightly uncomfortable. He kept brushing Kinzi's cock with his other paw, keeping him aroused, until Kinzi moaned more loudly and said, "I'm ready, I'm ready." As if Hayward couldn't tell from the size of his knot.

"Mmkay." When Kinzi opened his eyes, Hayward was smiling, his ears still askew at an adorable angle. He pulled his fingers out, and a moment later, Kinzi felt a larger, warmer pressure at his tail hole. He shivered, his fur prickling all over. "Now," Hayward said, "I haven't done this...in a long time. So tell me if it hurts."

"Okay." Kinzi reached up to grasp Hayward's paw. He hooked his legs behind Hayward's thighs and forced himself to relax as the fox pushed forward.

God, he was huge, twice as big as he looked. It felt like he was pushing his whole arm into Kinzi. But after the first stretch, it got easier. Hayward checked twice, asking if he were okay, and Kinzi nodded both times. He swallowed, trying to keep his tongue from hanging out without success. Hayward was driving further and further into him, filling him, pushing him back so that he had to curl his toes into the bedsheets to brace himself. He held Hayward's paw in his until finally he felt the pressure of the knot against him.

"Okay?" Hayward leaned over, his own tongue hanging out as well.

Kinzi nodded. Already he was adjusting to the size of the cock buried in him, the discomfort fading. He grinned up. "You feel amazing."

Hayward's smile lost some anxiety. Kinzi wriggled his hips, pulling them away so that Hayward slid partly out of him, then pushing back. Hayward got the idea quickly, matching Kinzi's movements with his hips, his shaft sliding all the way in, then back out.

Kinzi exhaled sharply through his nose, feeling the tingles of the movement creep up into his knot. He squeezed Hayward's paw, feeling the fox's shudders, hearing his gasps in the same rhythm as Kinzi's own moans. He was squirming himself, resisting the growing urge to grab his own erection and start stroking, so when Hayward started making moaning growls in the back of his throat, Kinzi pushed against the back of the fox's thighs with his next thrust. He could feel the fox's need in the tension of his compact body, the quivering with which he was trying not to thrust too hard. That was what Kinzi wanted, to help the fox let go, let down his walls, let everything out.

Hayward tried to pull out, to thrust again, but Kinzi held him locked close and pushed again, more insistently, pressing the fox's hips between his legs and his rear. He felt himself stretch further as the edge of the fox's knot entered him. "Oh...oh...oh, no, no, I, I, you can't..." Hayward tried to protest through his shuddering moans.

"All...all the way...swishy..." Kinzi gritted his teeth, his body shaking with the need for release. He knew it would hurt, but he wanted that closeness. He'd never tied with Hayward, and he wanted it, and he could see and feel that Hayward wanted it too.

"You can't..." Hayward said again, but by way of answer, Kinzi pulled him close, hard. Hayward moaned and thrust forward, wiggling his hips from side to side.

It did hurt. Kinzi bit his lip as the knot entered him, stretching him further than he'd ever been. He stamped the bed with his foot, but the knot went on and on and on, it was pushing his hips open...and then, with a pop, Hayward was fully inside him.

Things happened very fast after that. He was no longer holding the fox's paw; both of Hayward's arms were around him. The fox's hips jerked back and forth, unable to pull out or push further in. His whole body was tight and tense, wrapped around Kinzi's as Kinzi wrapped his arms and legs back around the fox. The large knot moving inside Kinzi pushed his own knot to swell further, his body surging close to release, just the rubbing of Hayward's fur over his cock almost enough to finish him. They rocked together, passion pushing through them in waves, until Kinzi really could feel their hearts beating together in time.

Just when he was about to reach between them to grab himself and start pumping, Hayward pulled one of his arms free and took charge. He was already making loud moaning growls right into Kinzi's ear himself, and as soon as his fingers closed around Kinzi's shaft, all the arousal and tension in the coyote escaped him in a loud whine, the soreness around the fox's knot submerged in waves of pleasure.

Hayward's moans became louder and longer, more like words now than guttural noises, and as the motion of his hips became jerky and frenetic, he almost sang his arousal. His cries echoed around the small bedroom, drowning out Kinzi's own moans, but neither lover could miss the other's climax. Their bodies shuddered, gripping each other tightly as Hayward pushed deep into Kinzi, his paw emptying Kinzi into the coyote's belly fur. Wave after wave of moaning delight coursed through them before they collapsed into each other.

Both tongues hung out of their respective muzzles, dripping. Kinzi recovered first, applying his tongue to Hayward's muzzle in a sloppy wet kiss. "Urf," he said, through the rush of warmth joining him to the fox. "Oh, swishy."

Hayward looked dazed, his eyes unfocused. Slowly, he turned toward Kinzi. "Hi," he said.

"Hi."

The fox was breathing hard. "He's gone," he whispered.

O-kay. Kinzi squeezed Hayward to him as best he could, in their awkward position. "Yeah," he said.

"I can't...I can't feel him anymore." Kinzi didn't know what to say to that, so he kept quiet. "He was always with me, whenever...whenever..." Hayward shifted, his knot tugging painfully at the coyote's tail hole. "But he's not...not now....I can't smell him, Kinzi, I can't, I can't..."

The fox's frame twitched and shuddered, very differently from a minute before. Kinzi held him more tightly. "Shh," he said. "I'm here. I'm here."

He couldn't tell whether Hayward was crying, but he was making small gasping sounds in his throat. His body shook in Kinzi's embrace, and Kinzi held him warmly, safely. The sounds and shudders subsided, slowly, as Kinzi's paws stroked his bare back. "You're here," the fox murmured. He pressed his nose into Kinzi's fur and exhaled. "I'm sorry. I didn't mean to..."

"You're going through a lot." Kinzi nuzzled him gently.

"Are you okay?"

He was already sore, and was going to be more sore in the morning. "I'm wonderful."

Their noses brushed, then their lips. Hayward murmured softly, "Can I just stay here for a bit?"

Kinzi smiled. "It's your place."

"I mean..." Hayward tugged at his knot. "Here."

"Mm-hmm." Kinzi tightened his embrace. "I might insist on it. At least 'til your knot goes down."

Hayward's stomach fur was pressed into the mess in Kinzi's, a warm stickiness between them. He didn't seem to care. "Maybe longer," he murmured.

Kinzi felt his eyes drooping. He searched for something to say to bring up the mood before they both fell asleep. "You know, I never heard you come without something in your mouth before."

"Feels good." Hayward's eyes were already closed.

"You have a lovely coming voice. Not squeaky at all."

Hayward gave a soft chuckle, rubbing his snout against the larger coyote's. "Letting it all out like that. You should try it sometime."

"You going to teach me?"

The fox wriggled his hips again, and this time Kinzi's legs twitched as the knot pushed on sore muscles. "If you'd like some more lessons."

Kinzi nuzzled Hayward, relaxing into as comfortable a position as he could manage while tied. "I liked the first one."

Hayward kissed his cheekfur. Kinzi let his eyes drift shut, too.

The next thing he knew, he was snapping awake in a dark room, his own musk strong in his nostrils, but not as strong as the scent of the fox in his arms. His warm, sore rear was now empty, but he could feel Hayward's sheath against his leg.

The fox stirred as Kinzi's arms shifted around him. He mumbled something and then yawned.

Kinzi stroked the fox's ear tenderly. "We should clean up," he said.

Hayward nudged his shoulder. "In the morning," he yawned. "Less you really want to." When Kinzi didn't answer, Hayward opened his eyes. They gleamed in the darkness. "Okay," he said. "Let's shower."

They showered quickly, together, since the stall was more than large enough for two. Kinzi took the time to run his paws over every inch of Hayward's body he could reach, appreciating it without the urgency of sex behind it. Hayward certainly cleaned him thoroughly, and appeared to enjoy it as well. He did spend extra time on Kinzi's sheath and rear, until the coyote spread his legs and panted in pleasure. Even the soreness of the tying didn't diminish the enjoyment of the intimate contact, though he did have to ask Hayward to be gentle.

While drying himself, Kinzi wandered out into the bedroom, looking around it again. The moon had come out, and in its soft silver light, Kinzi could see that the lower bunk's sheets were rumpled and stained. After the shower, their lovemaking seemed more remote; not quite dreamlike, but a memory of a night some time ago. Kinzi glanced at the upper bunk as Hayward, fur sticking out damply all over, padded in.

Kinzi'd seen Hayward naked before, many times. But there was something about the unkempt fur, the silver moonlight highlighting his curves, that was more real and near than any other time. Only the two of them shared this private world, a special feeling that made Kinzi smile.

Hayward returned his smile, a little quizzically. "We can sleep up there," he said, following Kinzi's glance upward. "It's pretty clean." He paused, and his ears folded down. "Let me just get one thing."

He stood on the lower bunk and reached up to the shelf beside the top one, coming down with a picture frame which he kept facing away from Kinzi. The faintest smell of pine reached the coyote's nose. Hayward held it close to his fur as he came back down to the floor, and stood with it for a moment before walking quickly to the closet. His tail was down, his shoulders slumped, looking for all the world like he'd been told to put the picture away.

"Hang on," Kinzi said. Hayward turned. "Can I see that?"

Hayward didn't move. "This? Oh, I…"

"Please?"

Hayward stayed still for another moment, then brought the picture over. Kinzi looked down at a photo of Hayward with the arctic fox, both of them smiling. His heart ached just looking at it, feeling the fox's loss. "What was his name?" he said quietly.

Hayward swallowed. He leaned against the corner post of the bunk beds. "Foster." His voice was almost a whisper.

"Don't put this away," Kinzi said. "I don't want you to forget him. You're the connection between me and him. I…I'd like to hear about him."

Hayward's ears came up, slowly. "Now?"

"Not right now." Kinzi looked around the room. He found a space on the dresser and set the photo there, carefully. "This okay?"

"Yeah." Hayward's eyes were bright. He walked over to Kinzi and put his arms around him.

"He looks really special."

Hayward sniffed. He made a noise and then squeezed his muzzle and eyes shut. He pressed into Kinzi's chest and finally managed to say, "He was." His body shivered as though he were about to start crying again, but after two shuddering breaths, he calmed himself.

Kinzi kissed the fox between his ears. It felt good to hold him there, swaying gently from side to side, their tails swinging in unison. He breathed in the smell of damp fur, Hayward's damp fur, and felt his heart thump with joy. Seconds stretched into minutes, until finally he felt his eyelids drooping. "Let's get some sleep."

Hayward nodded, but didn't release Kinzi from his embrace. His tail wagged slowly from side to side. "You can stay 'til Sunday, too," he said.

Kinzi's fur tingled. The warmth in his chest blossomed, stretching his muzzle into a grin. "I thought you said you'd tell me tomorrow."

Hayward nosed toward the clock. "It's 12:45." he said. "It is tomorrow."

"And past Sunday?"

Hayward bumped his muzzle up against Kinzi's chin. "Don't push it." His soft smile widened. "Come on. Climb up to bed with me."

Kinzi let the fox lead him up the ladder at the foot of the bed, watching the nicely-toned thighs and rear scoot up ahead of him. Up

near the ceiling, he lay on his side with one arm holding the fox tightly, Hayward's body comfortable against him, the fox's thick tail draped back over Kinzi's hip.

In front of him, the rims of Hayward's black ears glowed with silver from the light of the moon. With his eyes, Kinzi traced the bright outline of the ears, listening to the sounds of breathing, feeling the warmth in his arms and in his chest. He could do this. He could do this for a long time.

Between Hayward's ears, across the small bare shelf beside the bed, Kinzi could see down to the dresser, where the arctic fox smiled out at the room from a pool of moonlight.

Don't worry, Foster, he said silently. *I promise I'll take good care of him.*

He closed his eyes. A faint smell of pine brushed his nose, and then was gone.

About the Author

Kyell Gold began writing furry fiction a long, long time ago. In th early days of the 21st century, he got up the courage to write some ga furry romance, first publishing his story "The Prisoner's Release" i Sofawolf Press's adult magazine **Heat**. He has since won a dozen Urs Major Awards for his novels and short fiction (including one for *Bridges* and two Rainbow Awards (both for *Out of Position*, 2009), and continue to write in the medieval world of Argaea and the contemporary world c Forester University.

He was not born in California, but now considers it his home. H loves to travel and dine out with his partner of many years, Kit Silve and can be seen at furry conventions in California, around the countr and abroad. More information about him and his books is available a *http://www.kyellgold.com*.

About the Artist

Keovi is a popular artist and graphic designer whose work can be see at *http://www.furaffinity.net/user/keovi* and at *http://www.citralove.com*.

About the Publisher

FurPlanet publishes original works of furry fiction. You can explor their selection at *http://www.furplanet.com*.

WHAT ARE CUPCAKES?

"Cupcakes" are short and sweet, standalone novellas that fill the gap between a short story and a novel. In 2009, a trio of furry writers were lamenting the lack of places to publish novellas they'd written. Kyell Gold, foozzzball, and Rikoshi had exchanged their works and helped each other refine them, and approached FurPlanet with the idea of creating a line of quality novellas by trusted writing names.

"Bridges" is the first in the line. You can read more about Cupcakes, the authors, and upcoming projects at *http://www.furrycupcakes.com.*